# DON'T WALK AWAY

MONICA WALTERS

# INTRODUCTION

Hello, readers!

Thank you for purchasing and/or downloading this book. This work of art contains explicit language, lewd sex scenes, moments of depression/grief, mild violence, mental illness, and topics that may be sensitive to some readers. If any of these subjects are offensive to you, please do not continue to read.

This is book seventeen of an existing series of books, The Henderson Family Saga. If you have not read them, you will not understand who all the characters are. Character development happened in previous books of the family series. It's *highly* recommended that you read the previous books of this family's series (in order) before indulging in this one, because it updates family dynamics that I don't go into great detail about. The reads aren't very long, so you can get through them in no time. I also suggest you read the country hood love stories first.

<u>Country Hood Love Stories:</u>
*8 Seconds to Love*

INTRODUCTION

*Breaking Barriers to Your Heart*
*Training My Heart to Love You*

*<u>The Hendersons:</u>*
*Blindsided by Love*
*Ignite My Soul*
*Come and Get Me*
*In Way Too Deep*
*You Belong to Me*
*Found Love in a Rider*
*Damaged Intentions: The Soul of a Thug*
*Let Me Ride*
*Better the Second Time Around*
*I Wish I Could Be the One*
*I Wish I Could Be the One 2*
*Put That on Everything: A Henderson Family Novella*
*What's It Gonna Be?*
*Someone Like You*
*A Country Hood Christmas with The Hendersons*
*Where Is the Love*

Please remember that your reality isn't everyone's reality. What may seem unrealistic or unrelatable to you could be very real and relatable to someone else. But also keep in mind that despite the previous statement, this is a fictional story.

Decaurey and Tyeis were *nasty*! LOL! They had some real-life challenges when it came to trust and transparency. The ride, although somewhat dramatic, was beautiful. Enjoy!

Monica

INTRODUCTION

P.S.- Thank you, Author Mel Dau, for allowing me to use your likeness, name, and some of your reality for this book. I appreciate your love and support always, sis.

P.S.S.- Tyeis is pronounced Tie-EEES (like the direction east without the T at the end).

# Henderson Family and Friends Family Chart

## Wesley and Joan Henderson (Patriarch and Matriarch)

**Wesley Jr. & Olivia**
Nesha (W.J.'s daughter w/ Evette)
Shakayla & Chenetra
(W.J.'s daughters w/ ex-wife, Sharon)
Decaurey (Olivia's son)

**Jenahra & Carter**
Jessica & Jacob (Joseph's kids)
Carter Jr. (CJ)

**Chrissy & LaKeith**
Jakari, Christian, Rylan
(Avery's sons)
Janessa & LaKeith Jr. (LJ)
(LaKeith's kids w/ Nancy)

**Kenny & Keisha**
Kendrall Jr.
Karima
Kendrick (Kenny's deceased son w/Tasha)
King
Kane

**Jasper & Chasity**
Ashanni
Royal
Crew

**Tiffany & Ryder**
Milana
Ryder Jr. (Ryder J or RJ)

**Storm & Aspen**
Bali & Noni (twins)
Maui
Seven Jr. (SS)
Remington (Remy)

**Marcus (Wesley's son) & Synthia**
Ace (Marcus's son w/ Heaven)
Malia (Marcus's daughter w/Mali)
Seneda (daughter w/ Syn)

**Malachi & Danica**
(cousin of the Hendersons)
Malachi Jr. (MJ)
Deshon
Niara

**Kema & Philly**
(Tiffany's friend and Ryder's brother)
Philly Jr. and Philema (twins)
Kiana

**Shylou & Cass**
(Friends of Kenny and Keisha)
Shaydon
Shymir

**Vida & Aston**
Synthia (Marcus's wife)
(Vida's daughter with Jerome)

**Nesha (W.J.'s daughter) & Lennox**
Pregnant

**Jessica (Jen's daughter) & Brixton**
Pregnant

**Decaurey (W.J.'s stepson) & Tyeis**
Angel (Tyeis's daughter w/ bitch ass Kelvin) LOL
Pregnant

**Jakari (Chrissy's son)**

**Christian (Chrissy's son)**

**Kendrall Jr. (Kenny's son)**

## PROLOGUE
### TYEIS

"Damn, girl. Why you flashing all this body like this? You tryna seduce a nigga?"

I giggled at Decaurey's foolery, but it was an accurate statement. That was exactly what I was trying to do. The last time we'd seen one another, he acted like I was just a regular ass female, despite my flirtatious glares and behaviors. While they were subtle, they were bold enough for him to get the point, unless he was slow... like a normal man.

He slid his fingertip down my arm that showcased the sleeve of tatts I'd had done... a bunch of flowers and shit. My body heated from his touch. I was already feeling a way before I got here. My freakum dress was making a huge statement of its own. Somebody was gonna get fucked tonight, and I just hoped it would be him.

I had a backup just in case. Tyrese was my regular go-to when I needed to be tightened up sexually, but he wasn't relationship material. I wanted to be in love again. I hadn't felt love since I was entangled with bitch ass Kelvin, my daughter Angel's father. While I thought I was ready, I was somewhat afraid as well. I didn't want to fall for another fuck nigga that would fuck over my heart and make my crazy ass snap on his ass.

I glanced at Decaurey and gave him a closed-mouth smile. "I'm glad you're paying attention tonight. It's a shame I had to go to these lengths to get your attention."

He bit his bottom lip as he scanned my body. That shit was pink like he'd never smoked a day in his life and juicy like an overly ripe peach. I didn't know how they stayed like that because he surely smoked. I'd witnessed the blunt between his lips the last time we hung out. His eyes lingered on my exposed cleavage, and he licked his lips. This dress left little to the imagination.

It was blue with a plunge out of this world. I had to use double stick tape to hold this shit in place over my nipples. I didn't want everyone to get a show... just him. Blue was my color since I pledged Zeta Phi Beta in college. It was sleeveless and long, but had four splits, two of them up to my hips in the front, and the other two in the back.

My legs were exposed and begging to be spread apart for his light bright ass to slide right between. Just staring at his thick, pink lips and full beard had my girl juicing. I should've worn a different dress to where I could wear panties, because this dress was gonna be wet in the back.

"Shit. I was paying attention last time, but I just wanted to observe you and your mannerisms to see if you were cool or not. But shit, I don't even give a damn about that shit now."

His eyes finally traveled back up to mine as I anxiously crossed my legs. My clit was pulsating, indicating my pussy was ready to spit at somebody's son. I slid my hand over his beard, and that nigga closed his eyes while scooting closer to me and hummed low in my ear. I was about to detonate all over this cushioned seat in VIP. I gripped the hair on his face. "You keep humming in my ear like that, I'm gon' fuck you up right here in front of everybody."

He pulled away from me with a frown on his face. That shit only made things worse for me. He stood and pulled me with him as I glanced back at my friend, Jessica. She had a smirk on her lips as she watched us. I told her I was gonna get his ass tonight, since he halfway ignored my sexy ass last time. I knew I was banging, and I needed his ass to recognize and acknowledge that shit. I paid a lot of money to jumpstart my transformation and worked hard with my diet and exercise to obtain this physique.

When we got to the hallway where the restrooms were, he turned to me and pushed me against the wall without a word of caution. He laid his lips on mine, and his hands slid through the slits of my dress and gripped my bare ass. "Damn, you ready to be fucked or what?" he asked in a low voice close to my ear.

Between his voice and the bass from the music, I was juicing everywhere from the stimulation. I didn't verbally answer his question. Instead, I grabbed his hand and guided him to the prize while sliding my tongue up his neck. Decaurey had to be six feet or a little taller. I was five-seven, but with these four-inch heels I wore, he was only an inch or so taller than me.

He gripped my pussy and brought his other hand to my neck as I lifted my leg to his side. "This shit fat as fuck, baby."

He released my neck and gripped my leg. After withdrawing his hand from my treasure, he unzipped his pants and stooped. When his dick breached my opening, I nearly stopped breathing. "This what you wanted?"

I couldn't even respond. Decaurey was a thick nigga, and honestly, I wasn't expecting his shit to take my fucking breath away. I thought it would be nice from the print he was sporting earlier, but this was massive. He lifted my other leg and thrusted his dick inside of me. I noticed a couple of people watching as he destroyed my insides.

After a minute, he lowered me and put his shit away. "I had to get a taste, but I know you ain't ready for all I have to offer you. You just wanna be fucked right now. I'm past that. I wanna be in love. When you ready for that shit, let me know."

"I *am* ready, Decaurey. Just because I'm sexual and go for what I want, doesn't mean I only want to be fucked. I want that other shit too."

He stared at me for a moment then nodded. "A'ight."

"Are we gonna go somewhere to finish what you started?"

"Naw. I need to get to know you, Tyeis. If you only wanna be fucked, then yeah, we can finish, but I'll probably never talk to you again. If you want what I want, then we need to dial this shit back."

I wanted to slap the fuck out of him. When he pulled out, I was on the verge of cumming everywhere. Just the excitement of being in public and knowing people were watching had turned me on beyond belief. I grabbed his shirt as he tried to walk away from me. "If you leave me like this, fiending for my orgasm, you can fucking forget this shit... all of it."

He gave me a slight grin, then said, "You gon' get us put out this bitch. Come on, girl."

His ass knew just what the fuck he was doing by giving me the dick so soon. He pulled me into the men's bathroom and into a stall. Before I could ask why the men's restroom, he said, "Men ain't finna snitch on no shit like this."

In one swift motion, he had my heavy ass hoisted against the door and had me cumming all over the place upon entry. "Oh, fuck!" I screamed.

"See, you can't be screaming like that. I know this dick done changed your fucking life, but you gon' have to shut the fuck up so we don't get busted."

"Fuck you! They can't hear me over this music anyway. So, fuck me, and *you* shut the fuck up," I said as I threw my hips his way.

He frowned hard as he tried to break me in half. His dick was packing a punch I wasn't expecting, but I couldn't let him know that I could barely handle what I was asking for. He smirked at me, and said, "Make me shut the fuck up then."

He had the upper hand, and I knew it, especially as long as I was suspended in the air. "I didn't think you could," he said and fucked me even harder.

My pussy was definitely enjoying this shit, because she squirted all over him. "Mm, fuck. I do all that to you, Tyeis? I made that pussy regurgitate your words, huh?"

"You a cocky muthafucka," I said as I panted, trying to hold in my screams.

He actually had me listening to his ass. How did he do that? I didn't take orders, but his dick had me doing my best to shut the fuck up. His ass was dangerous, and I could already see he would be the one to ignite my crazy. That shit had me terrified suddenly. I couldn't lose myself again. Medicated or not, I knew I wasn't disciplined enough when it came to taking my medication to be fooling around with no demon dick.

"I'm not cocky. I'm confident in my abilities. Big difference. Now cum on this dick one more time for me."

My body submitted to him as I screamed out my satisfaction. The door was rattling like that shit was about to break. As I calmed down, I heard somebody laughing. "Damn! He killing her ass in there!"

Decaurey's face remained serious as he released my legs, letting his dick slide out of me. He gripped the head of it then turned to the toilet and released his nut without a sound. I didn't know what to make of that. I could barely stand, and he was all nonchalant and shit. When he turned back to me, he'd already fixed his clothes, but his crotch area was wet as hell. "Let's go," he said.

I cut my eyes at him and stormed out of the stall. Before I could leave the restroom, he snatched me up by the arm. "I gave you what you wanted, and now you wanna get an attitude with me... for what?"

"Because you're acting like I was just a random fuck."

"Tyeis, I don't know you, baby. Although I would like to get to know you, that was exactly what this was. You put the fucking cart before the horse. Now, if you wanna get to know each other, we gon' have to dial this back without letting sex complicate shit."

This nigga just called me a random fuck, and he was right. I wasn't trying to hear that shit though. "Fine. Let's go."

"For the record," he said as he wrapped his arms around me from behind then kissed my neck, "your pussy good as fuck, baby."

I bit my bottom lip, trying to contain my smile. I turned to him. "While you get to know me, you won't be able to deny her, Decaurey. I'll make sure of it. I'm going out of town next week, but I'm gon' fuck yo' world up when I get back. Put that shit on your calendar."

He chuckled. "Mm hmm. I'm gon' make you back up all that shit you talking too. If I can wreak havoc in a bathroom stall, imagine what I'll do to your ass in a bed. I hope you on birth control. I done had this shit raw. Don't expect me to ever put a condom on now."

I turned to look at him as Jakari walked in. His eyebrows immediately hiked up on his face. "You nasty fuckers. Wait 'til I tell Jess and Nesha."

"Jakari, I'm in good company. Now move," I said as he turned his lip up.

Decaurey didn't follow me out, so I went across the hall to the women's restroom to clean up. That nigga had stretched me to capacity and may have even split me a little when he was about to cum. For some reason, I knew I had met my match this time, and I wasn't ready to be handled. He'd put some shit on me that already had my mind running in circles. Hopefully, my lamotrigine and buspirone would keep me levelheaded because he was igniting my mania with his slick ass mouth.

That wasn't a good thing.

# CHAPTER ONE

## DECAUREY

Three months later...

"Had I known y'all was gon' get engaged so damn fast, I would have been pushing to get to know Tyeis faster."

Jessica frowned at me. "Why?"

"So we can have a double wedding and save this money."

She rolled her eyes as I chuckled. "Shut up, fool. Plus, that ain't her style. She all about her bag. Besides her daughter, everything else come second to that."

I'd definitely noticed that shit. Tyeis was always going on a job somewhere. She was a full-figured model like my cousin, Jessica, but Jessica had slowed down a bit. I supposed when I could convince Tyeis that I was the man for her, she would slow down too. This was my first time being with her since that night at the club. When Jakari called and told me Brix would be proposing to Jess, I knew she wouldn't pass up the opportunity to be here.

I'd been asking her to come down and chill with me, but she was so damn busy, she hadn't had time. I wasn't tripping though, especially since all this shit had been booked for months. We talked on the phone when we could, but I hated talking on the phone. I would much rather talk in person. However, I had to adjust to that, or I wouldn't have been able to talk to her at all. We FaceTimed a few times and texted each other most of the time.

As the owner of my own cement company, I had a lot of free time. I was grateful for that because it hadn't always been that way. I worked my ass off to be able to chill out. Up until a couple of years ago, I was working just as hard as my employees. Business picked up when my stepdad started using my company for the family business from time to time and referring me to people he knew. He wasn't a stepdad. He was more like my real dad, although I was grown as fuck when he came along.

My biological dad died in the military when I was only two years old. I didn't remember which war was going on at the time... probably Desert Storm or something. The fact remains that I never got to know him. My mother married some bootleg ass preacher afterward that I got to know as my father. That only lasted for five years.

He was pretty cool to me as a kid, but when I found out from my mom that he was sleeping with women in his congregation, I was as done with his ass as she was. I wanted to get at him first, but of course, she wouldn't allow that. That was when my mom's friend, Tammy, and I started getting closer, because she understood where I was coming from.

My mama remained single until she met Wesley. That was about a ten-year stint. That gave her time to recover from past hurt and truly get to know herself. She needed that time more than she knew. While Pop had plenty of shit he had to overcome, he turned out to be the best thing that ever happened to us. We gained a humongous family, including my sisters, Nesha, Chenetra, and Shakayla. I was closest to Nesha, though, because we were around the same age. We'd been in the family for almost eight years, and nobody could tell me I wasn't born a Henderson.

I nearly wanted to have my name changed to Decaurey Henderson. I didn't know any Franklins. I didn't know my biological father's family. My mama said when he was killed, they tried to keep in touch, but as time went by, calls became few until they were nonexistent. So I had no clue of any family I had out there or where they were located. All I knew was that they were from Louisiana like my mama.

I shook Brix's hand, congratulating him on their engagement as Tyeis hugged Jess and admired her ring. She'd met me at my place about an hour ago. While we weren't really committed to each other, I hadn't slept with anyone else since I dived into her reservoir. Her shit was wetter than water. I was hoping to get into her shit before she left day after tomorrow, but that had yet to be seen.

"What's up, nigga?"

I turned around to see Jakari behind me. I shook his hand and gave him a brotherly hug. That was my nigga. Whenever I went out, he was with me. We didn't go out without the other. Too much shit was happening these days, to innocent bystanders at that. We always had each other's back. I couldn't ask for a better friend than him. "I'm straight. What's up, dude?" I responded.

"Shit. I know we gotta be getting into some shit tonight. Nesha announced her pregnancy, and Jess getting married. We gotta celebrate that shit with just our crew, even if we just go to one of our houses."

"Yeah, you right. I guess it's up to the ladies."

"Mm hmm. I see you with Tyeis. How that's going?"

"That has yet to be seen. She just got here an hour before we got here."

"Well, do you think y'all could possibly take things to the next level?"

"Hell if I know. From our phone conversations, sometimes she was hot and other times cold."

"What'chu mean?"

"Sometimes she seemed like she was excited about getting to

know me, and other times she seemed nonchalant as fuck. She have mood swings like a muthafucka. I mean, she ain't never been disrespectful to me or no shit like that, but I can hear it in her voice."

"Hmm. I don't guess you brought that up to her."

"Naw. I still don't know her well enough for that. I asked her if she was okay, and she said yeah, so I didn't push. I mean, I know the particulars about her, but you don't really know a person until you spend time around them. They can't hide shit in person."

I glanced back to see Tyeis was still talking to Jess and Nesha. Lennox, Nesha's husband, walked over to us, and Jakari handed him a cigar. "Congratulations, man."

Before Lennox could respond, Jasper said, "Man, fuck that cigar unless you finna fill it with some shit I got."

Lennox slowly shook his head. Unc was fucking with him. Lennox was a detective, and he would definitely be risking his livelihood if he smoked a blunt. "He can't have that shit, but I work for myself. Save that good shit for me, Unc," I said to him.

He chuckled and reached into his shirt pocket, pulling out a joint. "Say less, nephew. Jakari, you want one?"

"Naw. I better pass in case I have to drive to Beaumont and be the designated driver for this fool," he said, side-eyeing me.

"Suit yo'self. Storm! Come sit yo' ass down and get lifted, nigga. You too uptight," Jasper said as he walked off.

Storm was still on his bullshit about being mayor of Nome. Election day was still a couple of months away, but that nigga was acting like he was already mayor. Marcus nudged him and walked over to the table Jasper sat at to get his fix. Storm ended up joining them. Everybody loved when Storm was high because he got calmer. If I could, I would give all his kids some THC too.

As if I'd thought them up, SS appeared next to me. He looked like Storm the most. He wasn't as rowdy as those grown ass twins and Remy, but the older he got, the worse he got. "Yo, I need one of those," he said as he pointed at the J between my fingers.

I frowned. "Man, go ask yo' daddy if you can get a pull."

He smiled slightly. "Y'all gotta always blow up my spot."

I slowly shook my head as Jakari said, "Carry yo' ass on, man."

He shot the finger at him and walked off. I swore, those kids were bad as hell. Maui was the sweetest. I didn't know how she was surviving in that house. She was seated by Ashanni, Jasper's daughter, and Milana, Tiffany's daughter. The three of them were extremely laidback... probably the most laid-back Hendersons in their generation. I watched Marcus's daughter flop on Maui's lap and embrace her like she hadn't seen her in years.

I wanted kids one day. Sometimes, I wondered if that was one of the reasons why God took Tammy away from me. I was sacrificing what I wanted to be with her. She was twenty-two years older than me and either couldn't or refused to have any kids. I wanted to believe that she couldn't after I learned of her diagnosis. I loved that woman with everything in me, no matter how sick it seemed to my mama. Tammy was her best friend and literally watched me grow up. She used to babysit me. I always thought she was a pretty lady, but by the time I turned twenty, I was fantasizing about her riding my dick.

It finally happened when I was twenty-three, and she had my nose wide open after that. One minute I was venting to her about some shit going on at tech school, and the next minute, she was face down, ass up. No other woman even mattered to me. It was like her pussy was laced with Fentanyl. She had me strung out on that good shit, and I refused to back down after that. The hard part was telling my mama three fucking years after that. We'd decided to embark on a relationship. Since it had gone past fucking, I knew I needed to tell my mama.

That shit didn't go well, and I went quite a while without talking to the woman that I loved first to respect the woman I loved second. When I found out Tammy was sick, my soul was crushed. Seeing her health decline was hard as hell because I could feel her life sifting through the holes in my heart. When she transitioned, I stayed cooped up in my place for a while, not wanting to accept that she was gone.

It took a long time for me to say she died. Transitioned just sounded better. It was like saying she moved or some shit. I still thought about her, and it had been almost seven years. Dating anyone had been out of the question. I talked to a grief counselor to help me through things. I knew my mama wouldn't be able to, because even though Tammy died, she was still pissed about the entire thing. I could understand her anger. I would have been the same way if I were a father and found out a woman her age was fucking one of my sons.

About a year ago, I knew I was ready to move on with my life. I was very selective though. Tyeis was the first woman to truly intrigue me. She was beautiful for sure and confident as hell. That face card never declined, and I put that shit on my mama. Her attitude though... that shit could change with the wind. I could sense that through the phone.

One minute she would be cool, and the next, she was getting offended by some of the stupidest shit. I told her in one of our phone conversations that I couldn't wait to fall off in her pussy again, and she flipped the fucking script, saying that was all I wanted her for. I got pissed and said, *"Well that's what you threw at me first. Had you led with intellect instead of that fat pussy, maybe I would want you for your mind."*

That really pissed her off. She cussed me the fuck out and ended the call. Then after an hour, her ass called back crying and apologizing, saying she should have just accepted the compliment, because I could be wanting someone else's fat pussy. I could only shake my head and chuckle. She was crazy as fuck, but for some reason, I was liking that shit. She brought drama to my life, and that shit made it interesting. Now if the drama started overwhelming me, I would be sure to let her ass know.

I kind of liked arguing about stupid shit. It could lead to some fire sex because the resolution of it all usually only took an apology... nothing more. However, with Tyeis traveling so much, our make-up sessions were on hold. Hopefully, tonight, I would be cashing in all those rain checks I'd earned over the past three months. I was backed up like a muthafucka.

"So where we going?" Jakari asked.

"Y'all can come turn up at our place," Lennox said. "Nesha has been having all day sickness. Different scents set her off. At least if she's at home, she can be comfortable."

"Shit, sounds like a plan to me," I responded.

Lennox nodded as Tyeis, Nesha, Jess, and Brix walked over to us. "What y'all plotting over here? I can tell y'all asses making plans," Jessica said.

"You always think you know shit," I said as she pursed her lips and shifted her weight.

When she tilted her head to the side dramatically, I laughed. "We going to Nesha and Lennox's house so she'll be more comfortable."

"Now tell me I don't know what the fuck I be talking about. Can we chill tonight and go out tomorrow though? I need to show my man just how happy I am ASAP."

Brix leaned over and kissed Jessica's lips as Jakari fake dry heaved. I chuckled as I grabbed Tyeis by the hand and pulled her close. "I feel you on that," I said as I scanned my baby's body.

Her cheeks reddened, and her slanted eyes narrowed as she stared at me sexily over her glasses. She puckered her thick lips, and I leaned over and kissed them, pulling the bottom between my lips. "See, that's my cue to leave. I can't take all this romantic and love shit. I'm going hang with the younger crew. I'm sure Christian and KJ will show me a good time," Jakari said and walked off.

I couldn't help but chuckle. I was the one that was usually pulling them out to a party or trail ride. Any type of turnup was my specialty. Now that Tyeis was finally back in town and actually making time for me, I had to show her that giving her my time was my first priority. She was always so busy I couldn't even go to Houston to spend time with her.

She constantly reminded me that getting her bag was of utmost importance since she was a single mother with a college student. I could understand that, but to me, it felt like she was crawfishing her way out of the shit she said in the club that night. It didn't seem like she was ready for the level of commitment I was ready for. However, after the way her pussy felt around my dick, I couldn't just let go without seeing where we would end up.

Now that she was done running from me, I was anxious to see how we would progress. We didn't have a commitment in place, but I was seriously hoping that we would before she left next week. She would be staying with me for five days before she needed to go back to Houston, and I planned to show her that I was the man she needed... not to just fuck her body out of its functionality, but to also fuck her mind into dreamland.

## CHAPTER TWO

### TYEIS

"So you know the date you told me to put on my calendar passed a long time ago," Decaurey said as we traveled from Nome to his condo in Beaumont.

"I'm aware. Better late than never though, right?"

I crossed my legs then my arms across my chest as he glanced at me. I wasn't in the greatest mood. My daughter had been having a tough time her first semester of school. Her mental health was of most importance to me. She didn't have bipolar disorder like me, but she was diagnosed with down syndrome before birth. Her symptoms were mild, and she was able to still accomplish things that most kids her age did.

No matter how mild her case was, cognitively, she was delayed slightly. It took her a little longer to walk and talk, but by two years of age, she was walking, and by four, she was forming sentences. Once she started talking, she seemed to excel a little more. Being her protector took a toll on me, but I wouldn't have it any other way. So when she wanted to go away to school, it was like someone snatched a rug from under me.

I never wanted to be the mother that treated her like something was wrong with her, and I refused to allow her to believe that something was wrong either. She was different... special. She was my baby, and I hated that my parents weren't here to witness her growth and struggle for independence. I wasn't ready to let go. Her wanting her independence made me feel like she no longer needed me. I hated that feeling. In my mind, she wasn't ready to be alone in the world. She needed me to look out for her and do things for her.

When she left, I cried like a big baby. She was all the way in fucking Washington D.C. at Howard University. I spent three weeks out there following her around to make sure she was okay. Seeing her thrive without me only made me depressed as hell. It was like I was able to hold my shit together because I had to be there for her. Now that she didn't need me as much, I found myself spiraling a bit.

While my medicines stabilized my mood swings a bit, I hated taking the shit. I fought bouts of insomnia, nausea, and unexplained anger all the time. When I found out they were all side effects of the Lamotrigine, it pissed me off. Then my anger was explained. I was in a cranky mood most times, so it was common for me to miss doses. The horrible side effect I suffered from the Buspirone was fatigue. So I was fatigued but couldn't sleep because of the insomnia. My counselor got on me all the time about that. We had a love-hate relationship for sure.

"You good? You seem a little irritated, baby."

I took a deep breath, doing my best to relax. Decaurey didn't deserve my attitude. "I'm okay. Just a little fatigued. I just flew in from D.C. yesterday morning."

"I understand. I'ma take care of you while you're here."

I gave him a one-cheeked smile as he grabbed my hand. He brought it to his lips and kissed it, easing my mood further. Decaurey could be so many things, from aggressive to funny as fuck, but I loved when he was sweet and sensitive like this. After our restroom fuck three months ago, he'd shown me that side of him when he took me to lunch the next day. He wanted to spend every waking moment with me for the rest of my stay.

I knew this trip would be no different. I was way too happy when Jess said she wanted to spend alone time with Brix tonight. For once, I didn't feel like turning up. I just wanted to relax and try to get some much-needed sleep. I wanted to believe that she could sense that coming from me. She knew my mood swings well, but I had never told her of my diagnosis. The fact that she understood me despite her ignorance of my condition only made me love her more.

I had never really had female friends, which was why I made a great human resources manager. Shylou loved my no-nonsense attitude and how I handled business. I was never biased because I didn't like any of those hoes that worked for him. That impressed him though, and I was elated that he respected my mantra: job first, no new friends. When he started his clothing line and he asked me to be a model for his full-figured line, I jumped at the opportunity.

I was still his human resources director until things really took off. I didn't have time to do it after that. However, I still went in from time to time to help out, especially when it was open enrollment for the insurance benefits. The more I worked, the more I was around Jessica. My mantra of no new friends went out the window. From our first conversation, I loved her. When I met her family, that love extended to them as well.

But this nigga...

Decaurey was gonna have me losing all my good sense. The way he was promising to cater to me had me feeling soft as hell. All my worries about my daughter, my schedule, and my meds had gone out the window. Even my fears about being in a relationship with him had taken a break. I had been overthinking that shit. My worries about how he would perceive me, my illness, and my daughter had taken over my entire fucking life. That on top of my other fears had me extremely irritable.

Seeing him after three months had me feeling somewhat peaceful though. I knew this was what I needed, but convincing myself I deserved him had been hard. Plus, I didn't want to enlighten him on my mental state until he got to know me better. At this point, I felt like he could choose to not be bothered with me, because we weren't in a committed relationship, nor did he know me well enough.

When we pulled into his complex, he turned to me and smiled. "I broke ground on my house in Nome, so depending on how long you take to visit me again, this may be the only time you see this place."

"How long did they say it would take to build your house?"

"Shiiid, not long. About three months or so. They don't fuck around. I'll be moving in before you know it."

"Well, we'll see. Hopefully, I'll be back before then."

I smiled as he parked then got out to help me out. While I had been here to change earlier, I didn't really get a good look at things. The complex seemed nice from what I could tell in the dark. I supposed he would take me on a short tour of his condo once we were inside. Earlier, I saw his bathroom and the guestroom since he was cleaning his bedroom.

When my door opened, he helped me out of his Tahoe and right into his arms. His embrace felt good as hell. I moaned softly as I slid my arms around his waist. I loved his thickness. He wasn't fat by any means. I pulled away slightly and stared up at his brown eyes then traced the freckles on the bridge of his nose to the ones between and above his eyebrows. My eyes bounced to each one, then landed on his thick lips as he licked them.

I traced my fingertips over them, but before I could pull them away, he pulled one into his mouth and sucked it, causing my nipples to stand at fucking attention. I wasn't even horny before that. Now I couldn't see myself going to sleep until he graced my walls. Tyrese had come through about a month ago and scratched my itch. I'd been with him a couple of times since I'd last seen Decaurey. After being with Decaurey, Tyrese wasn't even that appealing anymore. Shit, if he wasn't stretching my pussy out, I didn't need him.

The only problem was that I knew Decaurey wanted more. He wanted my heart, but he didn't know that shit was on a defibrillator, hanging on by a thread. Bitch ass Kelvin had ruined me nineteen years ago, and the two failed relationships after that didn't help. I told Decaurey I was ready. That was a whole ass lie that I'd even sold to myself. I supposed that didn't even matter at this moment. I didn't know him well enough to commit to him, and that was intentional.

He pulled my arm from around him then grabbed my hand and kissed it again. "Let's go inside."

I nodded in agreement as he intertwined his fingers with mine and led me to his place. Once we got to the door, he turned to me. "I've been waiting for the moment when I would see you again."

He brought his hand to my cheek and gently stroked it with his thumb then turned around and unlocked the door. His tenderness had me so in my feelings I didn't know what to do at this point. Exposing my emotions was a no-no. It was something I hadn't done in years, but he was pulling the shit out of me. That scared me half to death.

When he opened the door, I walked in past him and went straight to the guestroom I was in earlier. After taking deep breaths, I turned toward the door to see him standing there watching me. He stood there in silence for a moment, then as if he were a mind reader, he asked, "What are you scared of, man? It feels like you running from me. Let me know if I'm wasting my time, 'cause that's shit I can't get back."

I lowered my head and closed my eyes, doing my best to keep the tears at bay. I couldn't even respond to him. The minute I opened my mouth, the tears would fall like a running faucet. I could feel it. When I felt his hand under my chin, lifting my head, I backed away. "Tyeis, what's up, baby? You flipped the script on me when we got here. What's on your mind?"

Lifting my head, I stared at him and decided to respond. "I'm afraid of being hurt. This level of tenderness scares me."

"So you'd rather me throw you against the wall and fuck you 'til you can't take it anymore? I mean, I can do that, too, without an issue. I just thought you needed tenderness right now since you were drained. I can be whatever you need me to be. Real shit."

"Why?"

He frowned as he stared at me. I couldn't focus on his gaze. I looked away and could see him tilt his head to the side like he was trying to figure me out. "Because I'm trying to get to know you and prove that you can trust me to have your best interest at heart. That's what people normally do when they tryna establish something meaningful."

"I mean... why me though?"

His facial expression softened some. The frown was gone and replaced with a look of concern. His eyebrows were lifted and scrunched together. "'Cause you feisty as hell and got a slick mouth... literally and figuratively. I like that shit. Not to mention, you're beautiful, girl. Fly as shit." He stepped in my space and brought his hand between my legs, gripping my pussy like it belonged to him. "And this shit right here? Like a first-class flight to Dubai, baby."

He lightly kissed my lips as he massaged my clit through my clothes. When he moved to my neck, I felt a shiver go up my spine. I needed him now. Pulling away from him, I began unbuttoning the jumpsuit and pulled it off my shoulders. Decaurey took over from there, moving slowly as his eyes feasted on the sight before him.

By the time he got my clothes off, I was wet as hell, ready for whatever. He took his time, kissing me in various places, causing me to fiend for the inevitable. This tender loving and attention had tears falling from my eyes, despite me trying to hold them in. I quickly swiped at them as he kissed the top of my tatted foot.

When he stood, he grabbed my hand and pulled me out of the room to his bedroom. "Can you sleep with me tonight? I need to feel your body against mine all night, Ty."

I nodded, and he smiled at me then bit his bottom lip and led me to the en suite bathroom. After starting the shower, he turned to me and began undressing. His thick ass had me drooling on myself. Once he was completely naked, my knees were weak. I took my glasses off and set them on the countertop, then literally dropped to my knees to be eye level with his dick. Sliding my hands up the backs of his smooth legs, I could feel the power they possessed. I shifted my gaze to find his. He had a serious expression on his face.

That threw me off. I expected him to be biting his lip or have his head dropped back in anticipation. Instead, he bent over and helped me from the floor. "He been cooped up in drawz all day. Let him get some air, water, and soap first. Then you can suck on him all night if you want to. I'll let you have your way with me, since it seems that's what you want."

He didn't say that like that was what he wanted. He seemed disappointed. I didn't address it though. We got in the shower, and he allowed me to get in front to soak up as much hot water as I wanted before he started washing me. As hard as I was trying to avoid his tenderness, he wouldn't let me. He was determined to show me that I was running from perfection. That was what it felt like. He was perfect, and I surely wouldn't be able to handle that.

He slowly spun me around to face him, gliding the loofah over my body. His eyes were on mine until he went lower to wash my stomach. Doing my best to change the subject, I said, "I plan to have a tummy tuck soon."

He glanced up at me. "That's cool, baby. I take it the loose skin is bothering you?"

"Yeah. It seems no matter how much I work out, the shit won't tighten up."

"How much weight have you lost?"

"Almost one hundred fifty pounds. I was a big bitch," I said and laughed. "I wasn't healthy. I had to get that weight off me to help me be around a little longer. My baby needs me here."

"What about you?" he asked without looking up at me. "Don't you wanna be here?"

"Most times," I said, immediately regretting it.

He stared up at me then stood and put his soapy hands to my cheeks. "Whenever you don't want to be here, what do you do to remedy yourself of that feeling?"

I pulled away from him. "Honestly?"

He lowered his head, but his eyes stayed on me, and that shit made me nervous as hell. "Yeah."

"I have sex, or I sleep the day or days away until something like work or my daughter's needs distract me."

He tucked his lip into his mouth and nodded. He continued washing me. "When my ex-girlfriend died, I thought I wanted to die too. I had to see a grief counselor. It helped a little, but I didn't truly get better until I wanted to get better."

"Well, I'm glad you got better," I said, backing under the spray.

He stared at me too hard. I knew he was trying to figure me out without asking questions, but he never would unless he had experience with bipolar depression. He'd told me about his ex, and never once did he mention she was mentally ill. He'd been transparent about everything. I was the one keeping him at arm's length, not wanting him to get too close.

"You don't want to be better, Ty?"

Once I was done rinsing off, I left him in the shower to figure the shit out on his own. I wanted to be better, but my condition wasn't curable, unfortunately. Had he known that, he wouldn't have asked that question, so that was my fault. I did my best not to have an attitude about his question.

After drying off, I went back to the guestroom, despite telling him that I would sleep with him. I was going to have to get my emotions together soon before I fucked around and ended up telling him. I didn't take my meds today, but I would surely have to take them in the morning so I wouldn't snap on his ass.

## CHAPTER THREE

### DECAUREY

I didn't know what the fuck was up with Tyeis, but her mood was all over the place. The only thing she seemed to want was sex. No connection, just sex. I didn't understand at all. I was doing my best to be tender and show her everything I could provide emotionally as her man, but she was about to make me fucking blow up in this bitch.

After I finished washing my body and drying off, I walked through the house naked. I was finna fuck her world up since it seemed that was all she wanted. She lied to me about wanting more. All the shit I had planned for the next four days was canceled. She could go home tomorrow for all I was concerned.

I made sure the doors were locked then made my way to the guestroom. I flung the door open to find her lying in the bed butt ass naked, like she was expecting me. Something was wrong with her ass. I crossed the room in record time and rolled her over, pulling her ass up to me. I dropped spit where it needed to be and pushed inside of her. I wasn't even in the mood for foreplay anymore. Once I got my nut, I was going back to my room and sleeping by my damn self.

She screamed out in passion, and just like I did at the club, I gripped her neck. "Shut the fuck up. I don't even wanna hear that shit right now."

Her pussy got wetter with my words. I wasn't who she wanted. I wasn't a hood nigga with the woman I wanted. If that was who she wanted me to be, she was barking up the wrong fucking tree. I was only that way with hoes and people I didn't know. Although I still didn't know a lot about her, I knew too much to classify her as a ho. She tried to turn to look at me, but I shoved her head to the bed and fucked her like her pussy owed me something.

I was pissed. She'd wasted my fucking time. She knew what I wanted. I made that shit clear from jump. If she didn't want that, she should have been honest and said so. I still would have fucked her up. Knowing how good her pussy was, I probably would have dipped back until I found the woman I was meant for.

Her muffled cries were only further pissing me off. I slapped her ass and gripped it as I tore her cervix to shreds. When I felt my nut rising, I pulled out of her and shot it all over her ass. As soon as I was done, I stood from the bed to go clean up. I went back to the room she was in and wiped her ass and back then left the towel with her.

Going back to my room, I was still angry. I didn't know what was up with her, but I wasn't about to hang around and find out. I started getting dressed to go to Jasper's house. He would surely have what I needed to calm my ass down. When I left my room to go tell her I was leaving, she was standing in the hallway. She scanned me from head to toe. "I'll be back. I need to get some air."

I walked away before she could respond and slammed the door. By the time I got in my SUV, my phone was ringing. When I saw it was Tyeis, I refused to answer. She left a voicemail then I received a text message. Before I left, I decided to read the text to see if it would make me go back inside. *I won't be here when you get back.*

That only further pissed me off. I quickly responded. *Do what the fuck you gotta do then.*

It wasn't like she was stranded. She'd driven her car straight to my place. I was done begging her to be with me. She could kiss my ass now. While my mind was thinking that shit, my heart was trying to figure out what was up with her. Just from phone conversations, I could sense that she was moody, but this shit was beyond moodiness.

I peeled out of the parking lot, heading back to Nome to chill with my pop and his brothers. They'd all said they would be going to Jasper's after they left the barn. I could use some advice about what was going on with Tyeis. I probably should have just called Jess, but that was her friend, and she would probably make excuses for her. I wanted to believe if she knew something more, she would have warned me. We were family.

When I got to Jasper's, I could see the smoke from the road. I slowly shook my head, but a smile made its way to my lips. Before I could even get out of my vehicle, my phone was ringing. *Tyeis*. I silenced the call and got out. I didn't feel like arguing with her over some shit that shouldn't have been an argument at all. I wasn't about to stay somewhere I wasn't wanted, even my own place. I was too much of a gentleman to make her leave tonight.

She left another voicemail. I rolled my eyes as I made my way to the backyard. I already knew those voicemails were gonna probably have me wanting to choke her ass. When I walked around the fence, all eyes were on me. Jasper smiled. "What's up, nephew? What'chu doing here?"

"Tyeis giving him the fucking blues," Storm said.

I frowned. He was always in somebody's business. I knew he didn't know a thing, but he was saying that so I could give him more details. He thought he was slick, but everybody knew that shit about him. I slapped Jasper's hand as Pop made his way to me. He slapped my hand and pulled me in for a hug. "You good, D?" he asked.

I trusted W.J. Henderson with everything in me, and I knew he would give me good advice. I needed a blunt for now though. "We'll talk in a minute. I need to smoke right now."

He patted my back as Jasper handed me the tray to roll my own shit. He knew I liked to do that. For some reason, the process gave me peace. It calmed my nerves and inner turmoil. I gutted out the cigar and filled it with that good shit, then sealed it. The second I lit it, Storm said, "I was watching her at the barn. Something is up with her. She couldn't sit still."

I glanced over at him but kept smoking. He was the last person I wanted to talk to about shit, because if Tyeis said something foul to him, he would throw it back in her face. I could almost see Marcus doing that shit too. Everyone else could be trusted, but there was no way they wouldn't take offense to me saying I needed to talk to everybody but Storm and Marcus. I almost choked on the smoke thinking about what his face would look like if I said some shit like that.

"I think she may have issues like Synna used to have. I'm not saying she was raped or anything like that, but she may be dealing with some extreme trauma or something," Marcus added, speaking of his wife.

"Whatever it is, it has to be heavy," Jasper added.

Uncle Carter was sitting there smoking, and I could tell he knew some shit. Tyeis worked for him and Shylou. He and Aunt Jenahra were always at Mama and Pop's house, so he and I got to talk a lot more than I did to any of my other uncles. When I moved to Nome, I knew all of that would change. I would probably hang with Jasper more for obvious reasons. He was the most chill out of everybody. Kenny was chill too, but he was too quiet.

They went on to the next subject while I smoked, trying to analyze my actions like I was the one who'd done something wrong. I knew I hadn't done a thing. She needed to talk to me. I wasn't a fucking mind reader. If it was something I was doing that she didn't like, she should have said so. She said she was afraid, but that was still no reason for her to treat me the way she was treating me. I could see that being an excuse for not wanting to commit, but shit.

When I finished, I was lit like a muthafucka. I'd rolled it fat as hell. Pop tilted his head for me to go inside the house. I followed him, and so did Uncle Carter. I only called the older ones uncle, more so out of respect. Since I didn't grow up around them, it was hard to refer to Storm, Jasper, and Marcus as uncle. They were as off the chain as I could be at times, and they were closer to my age.

Once inside, we sat on the couch. "This is obviously about Tyeis since I know she's staying with you while she's in town," Pop said.

"Yeah. I've been trying my best to be a gentleman and show her my tender side. She said she was tired, so I wanted to cater to her and be what I thought she needed. In response, she gave me the cold shoulder and attitude I didn't deserve instead of talking to me. It seems she only wants sex, although she told me she wanted the things I did. I suppose some shit done changed in the past three months that she hasn't made me aware of."

Pop frowned. "So she doesn't want you to be tender with her?"

"No. She wanted me to rough her up and tell her to shut the fuck up. I don't have a problem with that, but she's not communicating. When I ask questions or try to make conversation, she flips the script on me. Left me in the shower and went to the guestroom after she'd already agreed she'd sleep in bed with me. I mean... I just don't understand what's going on with her. She texted me and said she wouldn't be there when I got back."

"She has something going on, but I'm not sure what. Shylou definitely knows. I've witnessed him calming her down before. I don't even think Jess knows. She'd gotten into it with another model and was about to drag the fuck out of her. He was somehow able to talk her down," Uncle Carter said. "Maybe I can ask him what's up with her. Storm was right about her behavior earlier at the barn."

My phone chimed, and I rolled my eyes. Pulling it out of my pocket, I saw an extremely long text that I didn't feel like reading, but at the end, I saw the words, *I'm sorry, Decaurey.* She ended it with a crying face. As angry as she had me, I was sitting here feeling sorry for her. "She just sent this long ass text, but she apologized at the end. Maybe she's ready to talk. I'm gonna head back home."

"Okay, son. Don't get caught up in no bullshit. If you have to leave again, do that," Pop said.

I appreciated him more than he knew. He was the father I always wanted while growing up. I was grateful to have him now. "Yes, sir."

I slapped his hand and Uncle Carter's then walked out to the deck where everyone else was. "Uh oh. He leaving. She must've duped him into thinking she was sorry," Marcus said. "Been there, done that."

Storm and Jasper laughed, and I laughed sarcastically and shot them the finger. They were more like brothers to me instead of uncles. I slowly shook my head at their foolery as I made my way to my SUV. Once inside, I opened the text to read it in its entirety.

*I'm ready to talk. I'm just so guarded. I don't know how to let people in. My daughter is having a tough time adjusting at college. She has down syndrome. While it's mild, she still has cognitive issues. She insisted she could handle it despite my attempts to get her to stay close. I'm always worried about her. Knowing that she is out there alone is tearing me apart. I've always been her protector. It has been just as hard for me, adjusting to her not being here. I let my stress and worry cause me to act irrationally. I'm so sorry, Decaurey. Please come back home so we can talk.*

I took a deep breath and started the engine to head back to Beaumont. I was burning a lot of fucking gas. Two trips to Nome in one day had definitely moved my gas needle. While I wasn't hurting for money, that didn't mean I wanted to spend it on gas. Tyeis's text had me melting like butter in a damn hot skillet. I was so angry when I left, but now I was feeling all sympathetic and shit. I had no idea her daughter had down syndrome. That was the most personal information she'd ever shared with me.

She didn't trust me. I wondered what changed to make her reveal that to me. She seemed pretty adamant about keeping shit to herself. I thought about her reasoning for the entire thirty-minute drive home. When I got there and unlocked the door, the chain was on. She peeked through the crack and slowly closed the door back and took the chain off.

"I'm sorry. I was just being cautious since I was here alone."

"This is a pretty peaceful neighborhood."

She nodded. I walked past her to the kitchen to get a drink. I pulled the Grey Goose from the shelf as she stepped into my space. "Your eyes are kind of low," she said.

"Mm hmm."

I poured my drink over some ice with lemonade and took a sip. When I turned to her, she looked nervous. Leaning against the countertop, I asked, "Why didn't you tell me about your daughter? You didn't think I would understand?"

"I'm just extremely guarded. Her own father isn't involved in her life. So, I assume the job of being her protector, and sometimes, I go overboard."

She seemed so mild right now, so I knew it was the perfect time to ask the questions I wanted to get answers to. "Is that the only thing that's worrying you? You said earlier in so many words that there are times you don't want to live. I just want to understand what's up with you and how you're feeling. That way when you snap on me, I won't take it so personally."

She fidgeted slightly. "There's nothing more... just me missing my baby and constantly worrying about her."

I took a sip of my drink as I watched her continue to fidget. She was lying. There was definitely more, but I wouldn't push. What Uncle Carter told me wasn't for me to share with her. I just hoped Shylou would be willing to share whatever it was with me or at least convince her to tell me.

I set my glass on the countertop. "Com'ere, Tyeis."

She hesitantly came to me in her nightshirt. When she got within reach, I pulled her closer and kissed her forehead then lifted her and set her on the countertop as she giggled. I stood between her legs and slid my hands along the sides of them. "You can trust me. I can't wait to meet your daughter one day. I'm sure she's beautiful and a joy to be around. I'm not a superficial nigga. You'd have to look like a fucking gremlin for me to have some shit to say about your looks."

She laughed, and that sound was beautiful. I hadn't heard her laugh in a while. She leaned over and kissed my lips. "You forgive me?"

"Uh huh, but you gon' have to make that lil episode up to me. I'll let you tell me how you want to do that."

She slid off the countertop and began unbuttoning my pants. "I love the smell of weed, and before you ask, I don't know why. I just do. I guess because I don't smoke, it gives me a high feeling. I love the smell of alcohol too," she said right before she slid her tongue across my bottom lip.

I slid my hands to her ass and lifted it. That shit was so damn soft. I kissed her lips and savored the moment like it would be the last time. I sucked her bottom lip gently until she pulled away to go to her knees. She licked my dick from the base to the tip then started sucking the head like it was oozing honey. I slid my hand through her hair and closed my eyes as I enjoyed the feel of those DSLs wrapped around my shit. "Mm, yeah, Ty. Shit," I said in a low voice.

She hummed on my dick right before it graced the back of her throat, and my knees nearly buckled. My legs were getting weak as hell, and I knew my nut was on its way. Tyeis applied more suction, and it felt like all the blood in my body went to my dick. "I'm about to nut. Shit!"

She sucked with even more enthusiasm, and when I released, she slurped my shit up without wasting a drop. She released me and stood, taking off her nightshirt in the process. I brought her back to the countertop and tongue kissed the fuck out of her. I needed to taste and feel her sooner than right now. I scooped her up from the countertop and headed straight to my bedroom. She would be apologizing all night if I had anything to do with it.

## CHAPTER FOUR

### TYEIS

Had someone told me I could get tired of a nigga eating my pussy, I would have called them a liar. Decaurey had been between my legs for thirty minutes. I'd orgasmed three times already, and the nigga wanted more. I was so fucking drained I felt lightheaded, like I would pass out at any minute.

"I'm sorry, baby," he said as he lifted his head. "Your pussy tastes so damn good you ought to bottle this shit up and sell it. You'd make a fucking killing."

I wanted to laugh, but he was serious as hell. He went up on his knees for a moment and stroked his already hard dick as I watched. When he hovered over me, he stared at me for a few seconds, watching me squirm in anticipation. It was like he got off on watching me fiend for it. He pushed inside of me, and my eyes rolled to the back of my head. I was in paradise. He was stroking me slow and steady, summoning my orgasm from me.

Lifting my leg, he licked from behind my knee to my toes then began sucking them one at a time. I came immediately. When my body began trembling, he picked up the pace of his assault and pushed my leg closer to my shoulder. Grabbing my other leg, he pushed it toward my shoulder as well. I scooted, trying to get away from him.

He stared at me until I said, "Give me more time to adjust. You have too much dick for that."

He smirked at me. "You can't make me wait three months if you need time to adjust, Tyeis. We'll be starting over every time. Your other nigga can't walk in my shoes."

My eyebrows lifted slightly as he stroked me with more power. I screamed out in ecstasy as I came all over his dick once again. I couldn't be fucking around with Decaurey, having mood swings and shit. His dick was a weapon of mass destruction, and he was using it to enforce corporal punishment. I swore I saw blood when I wiped my coochie last time. Hopefully that wouldn't be the case this time.

"Decaurey! Fuck!"

"Ty, I have neighbors. As sexy as that shit is, you gon' have these people calling the cops on us. When I get closer to moving, you can make all the noise you want."

Just as I was about to smile, he turned me to my side and slapped my ass as he slowly stroked me. This was a new position, so I was grateful he was taking it slow. He leaned over me and pulled my nipple into his mouth. This man was gonna have me moving to Beaumont in a heartbeat. It was even better than I remembered. I'd been carrying Decaurey's dick in my memory for the past three months.

I just hated that I lied to him. That was the time to tell him of my condition. He said I could trust him with what I told him about my daughter, but me being bipolar was a different ballgame. That could directly affect our relationship and how we got along. Angel, although I didn't want to admit it, was a grown woman. It wasn't like she couldn't fend for herself. Dealing with me on a daily basis could be a hassle... a big ass hassle.

I didn't know how he knew I'd been fucking someone else. Yes, I did. As sexual as I was, there was no way I could go three months without it, and he knew that shit about me. Most of our phone conversations were sexually charged, and my days typically ended with me fucking myself if I wasn't in town to where Tyrese could take care of me.

Decaurey released my nipple and stared up at me with those sexy brown eyes. He licked his lips as he gave me more power. The frown that ensued on his face let me know he was about to do one of two things: either he was about to nut, or he was about to fuck me up. When his pace quickened and his stroke deepened to where I could fucking taste it, I knew it was the latter.

My mouth formed an O, and before I could scream, he gripped my damn vocal cords, killing any sound I was about to emit. "What did I tell you? It gotta be that South Carolina in you that think you can do what the fuck you want to. Welcome to the country hood side of Texas where that shit don't fly."

No, he didn't. I was originally from Columbia, South Carolina, and I'd told him that when he asked about where I was from because of the way I talked. He said I had an accent, but I didn't hear it. Their asses were the ones with the accent. I just couldn't talk about it since I was on their turf. He continued staring at me as he tore my pussy to shreds with that smirk still on his lips.

As he released his grip on my neck, I said, "I got yo' country hood ass, nigga. Fuck!"

He only fucked me harder. I didn't know where he kept getting more dick from, but I was finna throw that shit up. "You good, Tyeis?"

I could barely formulate words at this point. My eyes were rolling to the back of my head, and I swore I was about to have a seizure. My body started jerking uncontrollably as my juices squirted him. "Oh fuck, girl!"

I felt him pull out of me, and when I was able to look at him, cum was hanging from my fucking eyelash. His eyebrows lifted and his mouth formed a circle. I couldn't even yell in protest or disgust. He hurriedly got up and came back with a wet towel. I closed my eyes until I felt him finish wiping it. When I opened them, he was standing there looking like he would laugh any minute.

"My bad, Ty. Your pussy performed a fucking exorcist just now, and I lost it. I apologize, baby."

"But why it look like yo' ass wanna laugh, Decaurey?"

He turned red as hell, and when I rolled my eyes, he chuckled. "I mean... if you could've seen it—"

"You just better be glad I didn't have my lashes on. I'm down to my last two pair until my refills come in." I licked what had landed on my lips and said, "Plus, you also better be glad I like the way you taste, or you would've gotten fucked up."

"Uh huh. If you say so. My dick ain't lost steam. Come hop yo' ass up here. You still have making up to do," he said as he lay on his back.

"I'm finna break yo' shit."

"Quit talking noise, and just do it. You already know when you get up here, you ain't gon' be able to take it at first. That's gon' give me the upper hand. Just give a nigga his props. I got dick for days, and you love that shit."

I smiled slightly. "There you go with that cocky shit," I said as I straddled him and slowly slid down his dick.

My eyes closed, and my head fell back as my fingers went to my nipples. That upward curve he had going on wasn't no joke. I slowly went up and down on him as he gripped my ass. When I opened my eyes, he was staring at me. "You so fucking sexy, baby. I can't wait until you're all mine. Real shit."

I swallowed hard. "What's going to happen when I am?" I asked through my pants.

"Only one way to find out, Ty."

"Mm. Well, start showing me now."

He pulled me over and kissed my lips with urgency, sliding his tongue to mine. I didn't know what the fuck I was doing. Decaurey had me weak, and I knew I had him the same way. The difference between us though was that he was transparent and willing to divulge whatever I wanted to know. I was hiding behind my daughter's diagnosis to protect my own, and that shit made me sick inside.

---

"A ZYDECO BREAKFAST? This shit is off the chain. You know how to zydeco?" I asked Decaurey.

"Yeah. You wanna learn?"

"One day. I'm too tired today," I said as I cut my eyes at him.

He chuckled. "Ain't nobody told you to stay up there that long, acting like you weren't tired. Now your legs all sore and shit."

I chuckled at his crazy ass and shoved some eggs in my mouth. We were at Jen and Chrissy's Diner, and it was popping in here. Lil Nate was in here showing off this hot ass Sunday morning. He'd been up there almost two hours already, jamming. I wasn't the type to listen to zydeco music in my car, but I loved it live. Besides, the food was amazing, but I expected nothing less from Mrs. Jenahra. Jess had introduced me to her mom's cooking a while ago, and I'd been in love with her ever since.

That love expanded to anyone she trusted in her kitchen. Her sister Chrissy was a bomb ass cook as well. I noticed that Chrissy was in the kitchen along with some other cooks. Mrs. Jenahra was probably getting ready for church. It was almost ten in the morning, and we'd been here since seven thirty. As I was about to eat a piece of bacon, Decaurey held his fork to my mouth. I frowned slightly as I looked at it then hesitantly took the food from it.

I chewed slowly, savoring the flavors. It was so good. After I swallowed, I held my mouth open for another bite, knowing that I was already getting full. Since my weight loss surgery years ago, I still couldn't eat a lot of food. Just the two bites of his food were gonna put me over the top. "What was that?"

"An omelet."

"No shit," I said as I rolled my eyes. "What was in it?"

He smiled slightly. "Deer meat."

"Hmph. Not bad. Not bad at all."

"I told you it wasn't. You gon' have to trust me, girl."

"I can't trust a nigga that eat turtles and frog legs... not with food anyway."

He chuckled. "Whatever. I was right about deer meat though."

"Yeah. It was good," I said as Jess and Brix walked through the door, looking freshly fucked.

As if I was one to talk. Decaurey had me up with the damn chickens this morning. We didn't go to sleep until around midnight, and the nigga had me up at five this morning with my face practically buried in a pillow. I couldn't complain though. He was giving me some of the best dick of my life. He promised that we would go back to his place and take a nap before tonight's festivities. I hoped so. We were supposed to be going to a trail ride, and I planned to fuck the dance floor up. I wouldn't be able to do that if I was tired.

"Hey, y'all!" Jess said over the music as they sat at the table with us.

She leaned over and kissed my cheek. The girl was more country than a sugar sammich. All these damn Hendersons were, including Decaurey, and he wasn't even a Henderson by blood. She had on some brown cowboy boots like the temperature wasn't set to hell outside, with a short, pleated skirt, a graphic T that read, *Country wasn't cool until the Hendersons made it that way,* and a straw hat. I rolled my eyes as I read it.

"Decaurey must ain't do his job right if you still this salty."

He frowned as Brix laughed. "First of all, Bestie Jessie, I do my job every time I go to work."

Jess frowned as I rested my head on my hand, turning my attention to Decaurey. "You shol right about that, baby," I said, agreeing with what he said.

Jess turned her lip up. "I hate that Jakari told y'all that shit. Bestie Jessie. Brix, I oughta bust yo' ass every time they bring it up."

Brix licked his lips and scanned her body. She shut that shit up quick. Her whole face was red. "Uh huh. Somebody put that act right on that ass," I said.

Everybody laughed, except Jess. She rolled her eyes, but she didn't say another word. The waitress came to our table and took their orders. Brix ordered a boudin omelet. While I wanted to turn my nose up, I knew that it was probably good as hell. I liked boudin, but in an omelet? I didn't know about that. I didn't know about stuffed fried chicken either, but that shit was good as hell too.

Jakari walked in before the band got cranked up again. He had Kenny, Jasper, and Storm with him. These Hendersons were some fine ass men. Had they not been married, Decaurey would have had some competition. Jasper was the finest of them all. I liked my men a little thick. Jasper was the thickest of all the Henderson brothers, and that was probably because of all the bud smoking he did. That nigga probably stayed with the munchies.

Everyone was standing to shake Storm's hand. "Aww shit. This nigga gon' really be on one now," Decaurey said.

Sure enough, when he got to our table, he had a huge smile on his face. "Hey, Uncle Mayor," Jess said.

Decaurey rolled his eyes as Jess hugged him. I couldn't help but laugh at how Storm frowned at him. There was never a dull moment around them. "D, watch that shit. You know you can't fight," Jess said.

Decaurey frowned. "Who said I couldn't fight?"

"Nigga! You did!"

"I ain't never said no shit like that. I said I couldn't fight a gang of niggas at once when we were going to the club that night and when we were going to the trail ride before Nesha's wedding last year. Get that shit right. I know my limitations."

I laughed so hard. His ass had better be able to fight. There was no telling what could pop off when I was in the mix. I kind of zoned out while they talked and laughed, glancing around at all the people in the diner. People were making their way back to the dance floor and having a great time. As Jess stood to go dance with Jasper, my phone vibrated in my pocket.

I pulled it out to see my daughter was calling. Turning to Decaurey, I said, "Excuse me for a minute. I need to take this call. It's my baby."

He nodded then stood to help me from my seat. Brix and Kenny stood as well while I made my way outside. Storm had walked to the other side of the diner, cheesing in people's faces. "Hey, Angel. Hold on, baby girl."

She remained quiet until I said, "Okay, I'm back. Hey. How's everything going?"

"Mama, I wanna come home. You were right. I wasn't ready."

While my insides were leaping in joy, I hated to hear her giving up on something she wanted. "What's wrong? Nobody said it would be easy. I tried to warn you about that. Is it your classes?"

"No. I just hate being alone. I haven't been able to really make friends. My roommate is friendly enough, but she's rarely here."

She sounded as lonely as I did when she left. That was why I stayed out there for so long just to watch her. "Aww, I'm sorry, baby. I was lonely too."

"You have work to keep you busy. Plus, you have Jess. After the semester is over, can I transfer to TSU?"

"Of course, you can. Are you sure you want to wait? School hasn't been in session that long, baby. You can withdraw and start fresh in January."

"Really?"

"Yeah. I would never make you suffer when you don't have to."

"Please come get me, Mommy."

I could hear her tears, and it produced a few out of me. "Okay. I'm in Nome, but I'll get a flight out there for tomorrow. We'll have to drive back with all your things."

"Okay. I can't wait to see you."

"I can't wait to see you either, Angel. I love you."

"I love you too."

I ended the call and broke down in tears. I knew she needed me, and I hated that I let her convince me she would be okay. When I felt arms around me, I nearly jumped out of my skin. I turned to see Decaurey standing there with his hands out to his sides in surrender. "I'm sorry. I came outside to check on you and witnessed you crumbling, baby. You okay?"

"My baby needs me to go get her. She misses me, and I miss her just as much. She's withdrawing from school. So, I'll have to leave early."

"Okay. How early?"

"I need to get a flight out for tomorrow if I can."

"Can I go with you?"

I frowned slightly as I swiped my tears away. "You want to go?"

"Yeah. Y'all are going to need help getting her things together, right? We can rent an SUV and a U-Haul trailer and drive back. Does Angel drive?"

"Yes, she does."

"It won't hurt to have three drivers though, right?"

"You would really do that?"

"Yeah. I'm your man, right? You said last night that you were mine. If that's true, then there's no way I can let you make that trip by yourself. I was chilling for the next five days anyway while you were here. I have time."

I smiled slightly, not sure if him going would be a good idea. However, I hesitantly agreed. "Okay."

"A'ight. Let's get our things. We may be able to fly out today if you want to."

"Well, I know we were supposed to hang out tonight with the crew. I think she'll be fine until tomorrow."

He pulled me back to his arms and held me close. "You sure?"

"Yes."

I didn't know how this would work. Angel didn't really understand the importance of secrets sometimes. She was honest to a fault. While I wasn't sure if I was ready for them to meet, I knew I could use the help. I released my worries as I silently prayed Angel would be shy like she normally was around strangers.

## CHAPTER FIVE

### DECAUREY

"Now I don't want no shit out of y'all tonight. The last time y'all were all together partying, y'all left the door to the bathroom stall hanging off the fucking hinges," Jakari said.

"Nigga, shut up. Quit hatin'."

"Ain't nobody hating, but if I had to take a shit, I would have had to sit my drunk ass on the toilet without a door."

I rolled my eyes as Jakari laughed and Brix slowly shook his head. Lennox handed all of us cigars as he joined us outside on the patio furniture. "Nigga, y'all fucked in a bathroom stall at a club?" Lennox asked.

"Mm hmm. I didn't hardly know her ass back then though. It was only my second time spending time around her. She was all the way in and wasn't drinking."

"Damn. I can't believe y'all fucked in a nasty ass bathroom," he said.

"Nigga, we were standing. You acting like I laid her across the toilet seat or some shit."

Jakari and Brix fell out laughing, and I heard the women

laughing at the same time. We were at Lennox and Nesha's house, and the women were inside doing their thing. Lennox had barbecued and invited us for a late lunch. We were all still full from breakfast by noon, so he pushed it back to two o'clock. Mornings were no good for Nesha, so she didn't join us at the diner. She wouldn't be going to the trail ride with us either, because of the smokers. So we knew we had to make time to come chill with her and Lennox.

She was twelve weeks pregnant and had already had her first appointment Thursday before they made the announcement last night at the family barn. I was happy for my sister. If anyone deserved every good thing, it was her. She was always there for everybody, especially Pop. I'd heard stories about how he'd taught her everything he knew. I swore she was the only woman I knew that could work on a tractor. The way she cared for him after his suicide attempt was beautiful, even after the rift in their relationship. She said that was what brought them back together.

"Lennox, you want a boy or girl?" Brix asked.

"Of course, I want a boy. What man doesn't?" he said and chuckled.

We all agreed as we puffed. Glancing at the time, I saw it was four, and I promised Tyeis a nap before we went out tonight. I surely had to take a shower before we passed out. I smelled like a barbecue pit. We'd been outside almost the entire time we'd been here. Just as I was about to stand, Jakari asked a question that I definitely wanted to hear the answer to. "Brix, you ready for Jess's video shoot with Noah next month?"

"Not really. I mean, I'm ready for the publicity it could bring to Nome and to the stables, but I have a feeling Nate is gonna show up."

"Y'all have beef?" I asked.

"Naw. I've never met him, but I know Jess was really feeling him, and I know he was feeling her even more. It's just going to be slightly uncomfortable being around a nigga that has feelings for my wife-to-be. Plus, I think they slept together when she and I were having issues about my response to the help I got from the family."

His explanation made me realize that Tyeis and I needed to have a conversation about the nigga she was fucking. There was no way she'd been waiting to see me again. She was way too sexual for that. When I brought it up, she never denied it, especially since we were in the thick of things. That was a conversation worth having, because I didn't want there to be any misunderstandings about where we were in this relationship.

"Damn. I can only imagine how difficult that would be. It's bad enough you have to deal with Decklan when he's in town," Lennox said.

Decklan was Jessica's ex and Lennox's brother. I was glad I didn't know any niggas in Tyeis's past. Hopefully, I didn't have to meet any of those muthafuckas either. Since Angel's father wasn't in her life, I knew that it wasn't likely that I would ever meet him.

Brix took a puff of his cigar. "I just hope I don't have to fuck nobody up. I ain't beneath fighting. Jessica belongs to me. She's the love of my life, and I will chin check a nigga to get that point across. Hanging around these Hendersons got me hostile as hell too. They never worry about the police. That was always the kind of comfort I strove for."

I cracked up laughing. "Hell, me too. When I came in the family and saw all the shit they were into, I knew my mama had hit the jackpot. Naw, I'm clowning. To see how powerful and resourceful they are, is refreshing as hell though. Usually in these rural areas, you have to worry about police and white folks being all in your shit. They so well-known, I saw a cop look right past Jasper smoking a J while he was driving," I said.

Lennox twisted his lips to the side and laughed. "Must've been a county cop. The city cops be tryna meet them quotas, my boy."

I chuckled then stood from my seat. "Well, Brix, I don't think you have a thing to worry about. You got a good woman in Jess, and she loyal as fuck. If need be, she will put him in his place quick as fuck. I gotta get Ty to my condo so we can shower and get a nap in before tonight. We didn't get much sleep last night."

Jakari side-eyed me. "Good. That means y'all ought to be on your best behavior tonight."

"We gon' be in the woods. If I feel like gracing them walls on the dance floor, I'll make sure we're standing right next to you."

"Man, the fuck! I'll push y'all asses over mid-stroke."

Lennox and Brix laughed hard, and I couldn't help but join them as I shot Jakari the finger. We all slapped hands, and I went inside to find the ladies seated on the couch, talking in hushed voices and giggling. They were probably talking about sex. Nesha tried to play that innocent role, but I knew her bisexual ass was a freak. I overheard her telling Jess about a threesome they had one time.

She was a beautiful woman, and I nearly got caught up with my damn stepsister after Tammy died. That was one of the most embarrassing moments of my damn life. It took me a while to live that shit down. I'd made her extremely uncomfortable, and I could tell that it was that way for a while, although she would have never admitted that. After that day and we had talked, she moved on like the shit didn't happen.

They all turned to see me approaching and smiled. "You're ready to go, Decaurey?" Tyeis asked.

"If you wanna get that nap in, I figured we better leave now."

"Okay."

She stood from her seat and hugged Nesha as Jess stood from her seat as well. "See you tonight, boo." They hugged, and then Jess looked at me and said, "Bye, sandman."

I frowned as they all laughed. Tyeis pushed Jess to her seat. "You make me sick!"

Tyeis turned to me and said, "Sorry. I call you my sandman to her. Your complexion is the color of sand."

I rolled my eyes and turned my attention to Jess. "I can deal with sandman better than you can deal with Bestie Jessie."

She frowned, and it was my turn to laugh. "Don't feel so good when the rabbit got the gun. People in glass houses shouldn't throw big ass rocks, girl."

I chuckled as I grabbed Tyeis's hand, and Jess shot me the finger. "Only Ty can do that, Jess. Let me get Brix in here for yo' ass."

Nesha laughed so hard she started dry heaving. "That's what your ass get for laughing at me like that, heifer!" Jess said as she handed her some water.

Tyeis shook her head at their foolishness. "Nesha, it was so good to see you, boo. Hopefully, I'll be able to get back here to see you again soon."

"Thanks, Tyeis. Love you, girl."

Tyeis turned to me and smiled, signaling she was ready, so I pulled her in front of me as Jess stuck her tongue out at me. "Again, that's something you need to take up with Brix."

"Get yo' ass outta here!"

I chuckled as I dodged a throw pillow she sent flying my way. I loved our relationship, and I wouldn't change it for the world.

---

"SINCE NATE CAME UP EARLIER, I can't help but think about how he came out here with me to get at Jess that night," Jakari said as we watched Jess and Brix on the dance floor.

"Right. I remember that shit. You and Mal had to ride back with me."

Malachi nodded as he remembered that night as well. He and his wife, Danica, had joined us at the trail ride, and Marcus and Syn were supposed to be meeting us here. Synthia was closer to our ages, maybe only a couple of years older. Marcus was only about eight years older, if that. Syn liked to turn up at times, so Jakari invited them out.

"Why Brix think they slept together?" I asked Jakari.

"Hell if I know. I wouldn't be surprised if Jess told him that shit just to let him know that she had options. I think Brix said that shit like that to see if we knew something. He would be able to tell by our facial expressions. Nate and Jess weren't around each other long, but I think he fell for her. The way he stared at her at Nesha and Lennox's wedding, I could tell she had him by the fucking balls. He would have given Jess whatever she wanted. He seemed real cool too."

"Damn. Obviously, Brix meant more to her."

"Yeah. She have a lot of history with Brix. Had it not been for her father's interference, she probably would have married that man a long time ago. Plus, Decklan had her all fucked up. Nate caught her when she was vulnerable, so I'm interested to see how this will go if he comes."

"You honestly think he's gonna show up?"

"No. I don't think he's going to want to make anybody uncomfortable. He's that type of dude. He'll definitely call to see how it went though. I don't know if Brix knows, so I refused to say that in front of him."

"They talk still?" I asked with my eyebrows lifted, anticipating his response.

"Not often, but yeah. More of like friends. I don't know if Brix would be cool with that, though, since he thinks they had sex. Jess told me that he texts once a month to check on her, but they've talked at least three or four times since she and Brix have been serious. She said Nate hasn't crossed any lines and that they truly respect each other."

"Damn. That still ain't cool if Brix don't know."

"I know, but what can I do but tell her that?"

I shrugged my shoulders then turned my attention to Tyeis. She was having a good time out here in the country. She'd worn cowboy boots like Jess and some little ass shorts. She looked good as fuck though. After downing the rest of my drink, I made my way back to her. When I eased up behind her, she spun around like she was about to fuck me up. After seeing it was me, she huffed. Well, it was more like a sigh of relief.

"You good, baby?"

"Yeah. These niggas just bold as hell out here. The only man handling me with that manly aggressive grace is you."

I frowned. "What the fuck is manly aggressive grace?"

She gave me the look as she slid her hands up my chest. "Oh, niggas out here tryna fuck?" I asked.

She pulled my face to hers and laid those thick muthafuckas on my lips, sliding her tongue to mine. When she moaned in my mouth, I was ready to make good on that shit I told Jakari earlier. I pulled away from her and spun her around then wrapped my arms around her. Leaning to her ear, I said, "That nigga, whoever he is, better be glad I didn't see that shit."

"Don't worry, sandman. I put him in his place."

"This name is only about my complexion, right? Because the sandman I know of was evil and fucking up people's dreams."

"I promise," she said and giggled until "Back That Azz Up" came on.

When she stiffened, I already knew she was about to have my dick on edge in these Wranglers. Something told me I should have worn looser jeans and my tennis shoes instead of these boots. Women's hands were up all over the place and ass started bouncing and twerking, including Tyeis's. I stood still and just enjoyed the show.

Her ass was swinging side to side then she threw that shit in a circle. That did it. I had to grab my dick and squeeze to try to keep him subdued. When Jakari ended up next to me, I had to pay attention to someone other than Ty. He had a nice-looking woman twerking her ass on him. He gave me a head nod and wink, and I couldn't help but chuckle. I was glad he wasn't just standing off to the side watching us enjoy ourselves.

Turning my attention back to my baby, I gripped her hips as she bent over and slid her ass up and down my erection. I pulled her up and held her close to me. Leaning over to her ear, I said, "Keep that shit up and my dick gon' punch a hole right through these short ass shorts and go for what he want."

She brought her hand to the back of my head and slid her palm over my waves, only making shit worse. I kissed her neck then gently bit her. I swore it felt like she was jacking me off with the way she was moving. I wrapped my arms around her waist, feeling completely lost in her and what she was doing to me. When that familiar chill went up my spine, I knew my fucking drawers were about to be filled with nut. *Fuck!*

## CHAPTER SIX

### TYEIS

"Yeeesss! I shed real tears! Nezuko almost died! Oh my God! I can't believe you watch *Demon Slayer*!" Angel screamed.

I rolled my eyes as Angel and Decaurey bonded over Anime. It just wasn't appealing to me. When we got to D.C., Angel was shy like she normally was around strangers, but Decaurey had the type of personality that forced you out of your box. He kept talking to her until he found something that would make her talk. When he mentioned *Demon Slayer*, that was it.

When I called her this morning to let her know I was bringing someone with me, she literally shut down... like wouldn't talk hardly at all. Now, her ass was talking more to him than she talked to me. It felt like I was the third fucking wheel.

"Well, I didn't cry, but how in the hell does a demon conquer the sun? When she kicked Tanjiro off her to go save the people from Hantengu, I was like, damn, she finna die. Then they started showing those damn flashbacks of when they were little. They almost made a thug cry... almost."

Angel was laughing so hard as I taped her last box shut. I couldn't help but smile. I was happy that they were getting along. I was also happy that it was keeping their attention off me. I didn't sleep a wink last night. I'd been doing my best to take my medication like I was supposed to, but this insomnia was about to kill me. When I experienced bouts of it, I usually had a negative disposition, grouchy as fuck.

However, today I had to work through that shit so Angel wouldn't start asking questions and alert Decaurey of my condition. Tomorrow, Decaurey would be taking an Uber to pick up our rental and then going to get the five by eight enclosed trailer from U-Haul. As soon as we got it loaded, we would be hitting the road. We would split it up into two days, stopping to sleep in southern Tennessee. This evening, we were going to Ben's Chili Bowl for dinner. I was excited about that because I had never been.

Decaurey was excited too. All he could think about was that President Obama had been there. Although Angel had been here for a couple of months, she hadn't been there either. She said she rarely left campus. She was ordering food through DoorDash and Uber Eats and had only left campus to go to the grocery store. I should've insisted that she stayed home.

My mind was conflicted though, because the entire flight here, I was wondering if I should make her stay to get over her loneliness. I wanted to prepare my daughter for the real world because I wouldn't always be here. No one knew when their time would be up. It was my job to get her as ready as possible for that day. At the same time, that was my baby. I couldn't stand hearing her cry.

"Do you watch any other Anime?" Angel asked.

"Naw. One of my lil cousins got me watching *Demon Slayer*. What other ones are good? I don't know if I trust them to ask that question. I just happened to be at their house while they were watching it and found myself more into it than them."

Angel giggled. "Well, I like *My Hero Academia*. But you may like *Hunter X Hunter*."

"I'ma have to check it out."

As I stood from the floor, Decaurey appeared behind me. "I was just coming to help you up, babe."

"Wow. You still remember I exist?" I asked sarcastically, then laughed.

I was really happy that he and Angel were getting along. He laughed too. "My bad. We're getting to know each other."

"I'm just kidding. I'm glad you're here and that the two of you are getting along."

"Me too, baby. I was hoping I could find a way in. She's a sweet girl."

I smiled as I leaned back against him. "Mama, what time are we going to eat?"

"Probably in a couple of hours. Are you hungry now?"

"No. When was the last time you ate?"

I frowned slightly and turned to her. "I had a protein bar in the car before we got here. I'm okay, baby."

"I know sometimes you forget to eat."

I tried to relax, hoping she didn't ask about—

"Did you remember to take your medicine?"

*Shit!* "Angel, I'm okay."

I walked away before I lost my temper with her. She was only doing what she always did. She didn't know it was a secret or that she shouldn't mention it in front of Decaurey. He had a confused look on his face. I could see he'd followed me through the mirror on the wall. I definitely didn't want him having any more alone time with Angel, because she would spill fucking war secrets without an ounce of discretion.

When I walked into the bathroom, he stepped in behind me. "You good? What meds you take?"

He didn't waste any time before hopping in my business. I closed my eyes, and I took a deep breath. "I take medicine for depression," I said, only telling a partial truth.

One of my medications treated depression, but I still couldn't tell him the whole truth. I feared his rejection. Decaurey was a good man. We'd just made up a couple of days ago from when I almost destroyed us before we'd begun. I couldn't spring this on him now. I needed to show him that he was making a great choice by choosing me to be his woman.

"Why didn't you tell me? That's nothing to be ashamed of. I told you about my issues with depression after Tammy died. If anyone understands it, I do."

"I know. It's just always been something I was embarrassed about. I'm sorry I didn't tell you."

He pulled me in his arms and embraced me, gently rubbing my back. I felt so guilty about not telling him everything but not guilty enough to actually tell him. This was so hard. I took deep breaths and pulled away from him then brought my hand to his face and gently stroked his cheek. The way he stared at me was threatening to pull the tears right out of me. "Tyeis, you have nothing to be embarrassed about, baby. I got'chu, okay?"

I nodded. "Thank you."

"You don't have to thank me. I'm your man, right? It's part of the territory. You don't have to deal with that beast alone anymore."

He leaned over and kissed my lips. When he pulled away from me, I noticed Angel standing in the doorway. "Mama, you okay?"

"Yeah, baby. Thank you."

Decaurey's phone rang, so he pulled it from his pocket. He answered on speakerphone, which was surprising to me. "Hello?"

"So yo' ass leave the whole damn state and didn't bother to call yo' mama?"

"My bad, Ma. I talked to Pop, so I knew he would tell you."

"I'm gon' beat yo' ass when you get back. When are you coming back so I can make sure I carve out time in my schedule to deliver that ass whupping?"

Angel and I giggled as Decaurey slowly shook his head. "I'll be back day after tomorrow, Ma."

"You have me on speakerphone?"

"Yes. That way I have witnesses in case I come up missing."

I laughed even louder. I couldn't contain myself. "Hello, Mrs. Henderson," I said through my laughter.

She and I had met the last time I was in town, but of course, Decaurey and I weren't a couple back then. We had a short conversation at the family barn the other night though. She seemed to be a nice woman, but I could tell that she didn't take shit off nobody. Actually, I noticed most of the Henderson women seemed that way, except Chrissy. She was the nicest of all of them. Although Storm's wife wasn't a Henderson biologically, she was as mild mannered as Chrissy. She had to be to deal with Storm's foolishness. The others were nice as well, but that feistiness in them could be seen a mile away.

"Hello, Tyeis. I hate you had to hear my salty side. Of all the flavors out there, I had to choose to be salty, huh?"

It was evident where Dercaurey got his sense of humor. "I totally understand. I would be the same way with my child if I were in your position."

"Ty, don't gas her up. She already got a full tank, baby."

I laughed and walked to the hallway to give him privacy to talk to his mama. Angel followed me to the front room. When I sat on her bed, she sat next to me. "You didn't tell him, did you?"

I stared up at the ceiling for a moment then brought my gaze to hers. "No. He knows I take medicine for depression."

"You should tell him."

"I will... in time."

"Why not now? He seems to care for you."

"I want him to get to know me more first, Angel. He could choose to not want to deal with me anymore."

"Like my dad?"

I lowered my head. Bitch ass Kelvin hated that I was bipolar. When the doctor said Angel had down syndrome, he left. I wouldn't dare ever tell her that though. I didn't want her to mistake his cowardness and cruelty for her inadequacy. She was a beautiful and smart girl. Him not being in her life was his loss. So I told her that he left because I revealed to him I was bipolar.

She wrapped her arms around my neck and hugged me tightly. "It's okay, Mama. I love you."

I gently pulled away from her. "I love you too, Angel."

She was my saving grace. She saved me from myself. There were moments where I wanted to end it all before she was born. Since her birth, suicidal thoughts were few and far in between. I knew that, if for no other reason, I needed to live to take care of her. That was why I named her Angel. She would always be my angel. That little girl made me better. It wasn't until my doctor switched up my meds a couple of years ago that I skipped doses.

She gently swiped the tear from my cheek. I didn't realize it had even fallen. When her eyes shifted, I knew Decaurey had rejoined us. After patting my cheek, I turned to him and gave him a small smile. He returned it and said, "Ben's is calling me now, so I hope y'all are hungry. You know I'm a fat boy at heart."

I chuckled then went and grabbed my purse. Decaurey had told me that he'd lost nearly sixty pounds over the past couple of years. That was amazing, especially to say he did it on his own. He said all he did was stopped drinking soda, lowered his food portions, and started working out. Men had it so damn easy when it came to losing weight. I had been trying for years before finally making up my mind to have the surgery.

I was exercising, dieting, and taking supplements, trying to get the weight off. All the different techniques, foods, and other shit I saw online, I tried it all, but to no avail. Nothing worked consistently. When I first started exercising and dieting, I lost ten pounds then stalled. It was frustrating to say the least.

Angel had gone to the bathroom. As we waited for her, Decaurey said, "I wish we could have gone to the National Museum of African American History and Culture while we were here. My mama brought it up on the phone."

"Aww, me too. I was just thinking about getting to Angel. We could have gone tomorrow. Well, maybe another time. We can always take a trip back."

"Yeah, we can."

He pulled me in his arms and kissed my forehead. "You okay though? I could tell you were emotional when I came in here after getting off the phone."

I stared at him, thankful for his concern. "Yeah. I'm okay."

"I'm ready!" Angel said as she walked toward us.

I was grateful for that because I could tell that he didn't believe me. Had she taken any longer, he would have kept pressing, and I would have possibly gotten snippy. Decaurey didn't deserve my attitude. Hell, no one in my life did. He got us a Lyft, then said, "They'll be here in four minutes, so we better make our way out front."

We left out, and Angel locked the door. I could only pray that I would stay in pocket to avoid Decaurey getting suspicious about my behavior.

## CHAPTER SEVEN

### DECAUREY

"Shiiiiit! Yeah, Ty. Suck yo' dick, baby."

After eating at Ben's, we'd gone back to Angel's for a couple of hours then made our way to our hotel room. I'd been fantasizing about this sloppy toppy all day. For a while, I wasn't sure if I would get it. I could tell she was in her feelings about having to reveal to me she was on medication for depression. I wasn't shocked about that since she'd told me about having feelings about not wanting to live at times. However, that seemed to be the opposite of what Carter had told me. I didn't see depressed people having to be calmed down. Maybe I had it all wrong.

I supposed people who were depressed could be irritable. I just didn't experience that side of it. Social isolation and restless sleep were my main symptoms. I'd also gained weight during that time because of excessive eating. Depression could probably take on different forms in different people, so I stopped overthinking things and just enjoyed our evening. When I did, we ended up having an amazing time. I took pictures next to President Obama's picture and sent it to my mama to irritate her.

She'd been wanting to visit Ben's Chili Bowl, but just hadn't made arrangements to do so, despite Pop telling her whenever she wanted to go, he would be down to take the trip. She had no one to blame but herself. Her salty ass sent back side-eye emojis, and I could only laugh at her response to my antics. I could actually visualize her face in my mind, making that very expression.

The minute we got back to our hotel, Tyeis had fucking attacked me, literally tearing my shirt off me. Even though it was one of my favorite shirts, I was excited as hell and didn't even give a fuck at the moment. All I cared about was feeling my dick breach the entry to her throat. That shit didn't disappoint either. She was sucking my dick like that muthafucka was melting and she didn't want to waste a drop.

I gripped her hair, and that only heightened the experience. It was like me doing that had unleashed something erotic in her. She released her suction and slid my dick all over her face, and I was threatening to moisturize her skin at any moment. When she pulled it back into her mouth, she stared up at me and nearly swallowed my whole dick. I didn't know how she fucking did that shit, but fuck!

I pushed her off my dick and went to my knees and slid right between her walls. When I saw her roll her eyes, and not in a sexual way, that shit kind of put me on alert. "What's up? Why you rolling your eyes, Ty?"

"I wanted to finish."

"Shit, believe me, you gon' get to finish in just a minute."

She bit her bottom lip and allowed her eyes to close. I leaned over her and stroked her deeply as she moaned. Shit, I had to moan with her ass the way her pussy was squeezing me. Damn, she was feeling so damn good. I brought my hand to her neck and gripped it as her eyes slowly opened. "Fuck me, Decaurey. Pleeeaaaassse, fuck me."

I went deeper and stroked her harder as she moaned louder. Her nails dug into my skin, causing me to growl out in satisfaction. Her phone started to ring, and although she didn't move to answer it, it kind of threw her off. "You wanna check that, baby?"

"No. Keep fucking me."

I just knew she would want to answer it since we were close to Angel. I picked up my pace as the sweat fell from my face to her chest. "Harder, Decaurey."

I frowned slightly. She seemed so distant. Something about her wasn't right. Instead of trying to figure it out now, I gave her what she requested. I was hitting the bottom with every thrust, watching her body scoot away from me until her head hit the headboard over the bed. As I was about to stop to reposition us, she screamed, "Don't stop!"

I lifted her legs to where her feet could rest against the headboard behind her and wore her pussy the fuck out. I watched the show, which was only turning me on more. The pinkness of her pussy showed every time I was pulling out to dive back in. It was like it was gripping me with all its might until it was about to turn itself inside out trying to hold on. "Oh fuck!" I yelled.

Her clit peeked out of hiding, and I knew her orgasm was near. The head of my dick got extremely wet, so I pulled out, and she squirted all over my abdomen as she screamed out in pleasure. I dived right back in, being sure to get enough of her flavor on my dick for her to taste. When I felt my nut rising and getting to the point of no return, I pulled out of her and said, "Come suck this shit up, Ty."

She opened her eyes and frowned. *What in the fuck is up with her?* "Decaurey, really? You stopped fucking me for me to suck your dick?"

"Didn't you say you wanted to finish?"

"I don't now."

I frowned and stopped squeezing my dick. That nigga shot nut all over her. It was my turn to roll my eyes and get up from the bed. Fuck that depression shit. Something else was going on with her ass. There was no reason for her to be depressed right now... not with my dick kicking ass and taking names up in that pussy. I started the shower and got towels to set on the countertop. She was making me regret this shit with her.

We hadn't been a couple a whole week yet. There was no way I should be having second thoughts already. Actually, it had only been a couple of days, and this was her second episode of bullshit. I pissed in the toilet then got in the shower without going back to the bed to check on her. I could hear her phone start ringing again and this time, she answered it. I couldn't make out what was being said, but at this moment, I didn't even give a fuck.

After a few minutes, she got in the shower with me and just stood there staring at me. She was blocking the water. "You got some shit on yo' chest, Ty?"

"Why didn't you come back?"

I frowned and tilted my head slightly. She had to be high. She said she didn't drink or smoke, but clearly, she was doing something. There was no way she was sober. "Were you in there a minute ago?"

"Decaurey, I'm sorry."

"Naw. You gon' have to do better than that."

She nodded then went to her knees and slurped my dick up. He was flaccid as hell. I pulled her up from the shower floor. "I ain't talking about that, and you know it."

I wasn't even in the mood anymore. That was saying a lot as much as I loved sex with her nasty ass. I needed an explanation about what was going on with her. She could say what the fuck she wanted to say. I'd already exhibited more patience than normal with her ass. I wasn't for a wishy-washy ass woman. If there was more to it, then she needed to say that shit. Otherwise, once we got back to Texas, I would be done.

She fidgeted slightly then stared into my eyes, her bottom lip quivering. It was like she was begging me not to make her say what her issue was. After a couple of minutes, just as I was about to tell her to get her ass out the way, she stepped out of the shower. I slowly shook my head. I didn't wait six years to date to deal with no shit like this. I liked Tyeis. If I knew what was up with her, maybe I could have a little more patience.

After washing up, I got out of the shower and dried off. I was so irritated, I briefly thought about getting another hotel room. When I made my way out to the room, Tyeis stood from the bed and went to the bathroom. I took a deep breath and flopped in the bed. I decided to text Jess to see if she knew more than she let on.

*What's up, cuz? I got some questions about your girl. Hit me up when you have time.*

It was already almost eleven our time. That meant it was close to ten if she was in Texas. Within a minute or two, she called me instead. "Hello?"

"Hey, D. What's going on? Can you talk, or should I have texted?"

"Well, she's in the shower right now, so I can talk for a minute. She told me she takes meds for depression. Is that all? I mean, I get depression can be different for everybody, but damn. She moody as fuck and wishy-washy. Like she changes her mind about things within minutes."

"Damn. I don't know. I didn't even know about the depression. We're friends, but we don't get to spend much time together because we're always working, especially her. What made her tell you about the depression?"

"Her daughter asked her if she'd taken her medicine. She had to tell me something."

"Dang. I hate that. I didn't know, D. I'll talk to her and see what's up."

"Well, wait until we get back. We should be back the day after tomorrow."

"Okay."

As she was about to hang up, I heard Storm's voice. "Ace, who you on the phone with? I need to holla at'chu for a minute."

I rolled my eyes as she said, "Decaurey."

"Oh, fuck him. He ain't nobody," he said then laughed. "I need you to come to my headquarters tomorrow."

"You mean the diner, Uncle Mayor?"

"Same thing. Meet me at ten."

"Okay."

When she stopped talking, I said, "Tell him I hope Abney shock his fucking drawz and throw his hat back in the race."

She laughed then relayed what I said. There seemed to be a bunch of fumbling with the phone. "Wait 'til you get back. I'm gon' terminate all those fucking contracts we got for cement work in front of you, yo' mama, and tight ass W.J."

The call ended, and I couldn't help but laugh. That nigga was crazy. My phone rang, and I knew it was Jess calling back. "Yeah, Jess."

"Sorry. You know your uncle don't give a shit about shit that don't concern him," she said and laughed.

"Don't I know it. You're his favorite, though, because you act like that sometimes too."

"A'ight, sandman. Don't start yo' shit."

"Bestie Jessie, for real? You wanna go there?"

"Bye, nigga!"

She ended the call, and I chuckled. I couldn't believe she didn't know what was up with Tyeis though. Hopefully, she could get to the bottom of it. I plugged my phone up and turned my back to the bathroom door. I really didn't want to talk to her if she didn't want to talk about what happened tonight. That ride back to Houston would be quiet as fuck.

When the bathroom door opened, I didn't make a move. I could hear her moving around the room. I wasn't sure what she was doing, but I refused to open my eyes to find out. *Yeah, I'm petty as fuck.* She got in bed, and she scooted close to me. Her hand landed on my arm like she was looking over to see if I was asleep. She whispered, "I'm so sorry, Decaurey."

Her forehead met my arm for a moment, then she lifted it and gently rubbed my arm where her head had been. She slid her arm under mine and draped it over my waist then pressed herself against my back. Her hand lifted to my chest, and she began rubbing circles on it. Thankfully, that lulled me to sleep for real.

---

WHEN I WOKE UP, I didn't feel Tyeis against me. I turned over to see she wasn't in bed either. I sat up to look at the clock, and saw it was after nine. *Shit!* We were supposed to pick up the rental at eight and be to U-Haul right after. The bathroom light was on, so I got up and quickly made my way in there to brush my teeth and pack my personal items.

When I opened the door, I fully expected Ty to be in there putting on makeup or something, but she wasn't. She'd just left the light on. Surely, she didn't leave me here. I went back out to the room to see her bag and purse were gone. I immediately went to my phone and called her. She declined the call on the second ring, sending me to her voicemail. I ended the call and called again, only to suffer the same fate.

I left a message. "Yo, if you left me, let me know that shit so I can book a flight. For the record, if you did, that's fucked up."

I ended the call and went back to the bathroom to brush my teeth. Once I was done, I packed my shit then checked my phone. She'd sent a text message. *We got a couple of guys from the university to load the trailer. We left about fifteen minutes ago. I picked the SUV up at seven instead of eight and the trailer was ready as well. You seemed to be sleeping peacefully, so I didn't want to wake you up.*

I wanted to throw my fucking phone. What the fuck was she talking about? I was sleeping peacefully? She was acting like I had another way home. I called her again, and she declined it. I was so angry I was trembling. I got on my phone and booked a one-way flight, leaving in a couple of hours then got on my app to get a Lyft. I grabbed my bag and headed to the lobby area then called Jess.

"Hello?"

"She left me."

"What?"

"When I woke up, she was gone. I don't know how I overslept, but I woke up about thirty minutes ago, and she was gone. They are already on the road with the trailer."

"What the fuck?"

"Yeah."

"Damn, you cussing early. Who you talking to?" Brix asked her.

"Tyeis left D in D.C. Can you believe that shit?" she responded.

"Oh yeah. That's fucked up," he said, agreeing with her previous observation of the circumstance.

"Her car is still at my place, but once she gets that muthafucka, I'm done with her ass."

"I'm sorry that happened. I can't say that I blame you. I can't believe she did that shit. No wonder she's been single for as long as I've known her. Wait 'til I tell Daddy and Shylou."

At the mention of Shy's name, I remembered that he knew what was up with her. "Shylou knows the deal. Uncle Carter told me that much. Hopefully, he'll share that information with me when I get back. Even with as pissed as I am, I'm worried about them being on the road alone. That's a fucking twenty-hour drive."

"I know, but all we can do at this point is pray that they make it safely. I'm in shock right now. I knew her ass was crazy but in a good way. She keeps me laughing. I've never seen this side of her. Have you gotten a flight back?"

"Yeah. My car just pulled up. I'll call you when I get to the airport if I have time. Don't tell Liv what happened."

"Your mama? Why not?"

"Come on now. My mama is too protective. She'll be ready to fuck Ty up. I mean, I wanna fuck her up, but I won't go through with it. Nothing will stop Olivia Henderson from getting at her, especially since I didn't even tell her I was leaving. She said she already owe me an ass whupping for that," I said, trying to lighten the mood as I walked to the car.

"Oh lawd. I won't say anything. I'll definitely mention it to Daddy to see if Shy ever told him anything about her."

"A'ight."

"Be safe."

"I will."

I ended the call as the driver took off for the airport. Tyeis fucking Warner was gonna have to be in my rearview. I just hated that meant the same for that good ass pussy. That shit had me blinded. Her pussy had my ass by the balls for a minute. This situation though... I couldn't overlook it. Storm wasn't even this damn cold. Thank goodness I could afford a plane ticket. I was only here to help her out, moving her daughter. I was here for them. Just because I could afford it, didn't mean I wanted to spend it.

I'd given her the money for the U-Haul, just to do my part as her man. Tyeis wasn't a gold digger, at least I didn't think she was one. She had her own money. If only I knew what was going on with her. That thought kept popping in my head. It made me wonder if I would take her back if I thought the excuse was a good one.

I slowly shook my head as the car drove through the city to Washington Dulles Airport. Things with Tammy were nowhere near this dramatic. I hated that she was gone. However, I knew my relationship with my mama wouldn't have gotten back to where it was had Tammy still been alive. There was no way I would have allowed my mother to disrespect her, which meant that we probably wouldn't have come around much. Tammy was the epitome of woman. Despite what my mama thought, Tammy didn't set out to be with me.

Hell, I didn't set out to be with her. It was just something that happened. While I knew she was supposed to be off limits, I also felt like God put me there to help her with the transition. Seeing her deteriorate right before my eyes was hard though. I could still see her feeble body in my dreams sometimes. I would give everything I owned to have her back.

As I thought about her, we arrived at the airport. I thanked the driver then headed inside to get through TSA. Since it was a Monday, it wasn't as crowded. The crowds usually happened on the weekends, especially on Sundays. That was when everyone was trying to head home. My mind was going ninety to nothing, so while I waited in line, I sent Tyeis a text message.

*You leaving me was fucked up, but I'm worried about you and Angel's safety. If you have a heart, let me know when y'all get to a hotel and when you leave in the morning. Y'all two being on the road alone bothers the fuck out of me. I'm at the airport and will be boarding a flight in the next hour. I should be back in Houston by two-thirty.*

I would be surprised if she responded, but I was more than sure Jess would be contacting her to go the fuck off on her ass. I sent her a text, letting her know I was at the airport and what time I should be landing in Houston. I needed someone to know my whereabouts without having to tell anyone else what all happened. I was more than sure I would be filling Nesha and Jakari in once I got home.

## CHAPTER EIGHT

### TYEIS

"Why did you leave him if it's hurting you so bad?" Angel asked.

"I'm not good enough for him."

"Did you take your medicine this morning?"

I glanced at her, answering her question without answering her question. "He deserves better. I can't give him that. Decaurey is a good man."

"If you would tell him about your diagnosis, I'm sure he would understand."

I refused to say another word about Decaurey to her. She didn't truly understand what it was like dealing with someone like me. I didn't take my meds today, because I needed to be able to sleep tonight. We'd gotten to our hotel in Chattanooga and had showered for the evening. It felt like my body was ready to crash, but my mind was running a marathon that it refused to slow down from.

Decaurey had called several times, and I just couldn't bear speaking to him. I knew he was angry, worried, and probably hurt by my actions. If only my dad were here. He served as my refuge before a brain aneurysm took him away from me. Before Angel was born, he was the person who loved me without conditions. Whether I had taken my meds or not, he showed me the same love and grace. I missed him like crazy.

According to him, everything about me I'd gotten from my mama... good and bad. I had to chuckle at his revelation, because that was probably why she and I bumped heads so much. We were just alike. However, I would much rather have her in my life now than to be trying to navigate through it alone.

As I stared at the ceiling, I could hear Angel talking, but I wasn't paying attention to anything she was saying until I heard her say, "We made it safely. We're about to go to sleep."

I frowned as I sat up and turned to her. She glanced at me then went back to her phone call. "Okay. I will. Thanks... Bye."

When she ended the call, I asked, "Who were you talking to?"

"Decaurey. We traded numbers yesterday so we could talk and text about Anime. He was worried about us."

For some reason, her calling him made me angry. I got out of bed and went to the bathroom and slammed the door. I sat on the toilet trying to figure out why I was angry exactly. She had established a friendship with Decaurey in less than four hours. He was just that great of a person. I should've been happy that someone cared enough about her to befriend her. She never really had genuine friends. There was always someone trying to use her for what she could do for them... usually her connection to her teachers. Because of her disability, she was privy to information to help her along. Somehow, other students knew that.

Before I realized it, I was crying, wishing that I could live my life normally and not have to worry about how others reacted to me. Truth was, I was afraid of forming relationships for fear of rejection. I liked Decaurey so much, short temper and all. He deserved a woman that could focus more on pleasing him. I thought that I could be that woman, but the past few days, I'd proven that I couldn't.

As I wiped my face, I could hear my phone ringing. When I

heard Angel answer it, I could have choked her. I tried to be private and hold on to parts of myself that I felt were no one else's business. I opened the door, and she immediately said, "Mr. Shylou said to call him."

I calmed down at the sound of his name. Shylou and Cass knew everything about me. Carter knew some things, but not everything. However, Shylou was the one that could always calm me down. I didn't know what it was about him. Maybe it was that Houston swag. Cass was a firecracker, and she only got me more amped up. When I was feeling a way, she knew to stay away from me. One thing she had more than I did was self-control.

There were times when I couldn't control my actions, especially when I was angry. Shylou had kept me from totally destroying a bitch's face at one event. Thankfully, she worked for Shylou, so he could do damage control. I was so grateful for how loyal he was to me when I could clearly cost him his squeaky-clean, lowkey reputation. The industry could label his entire company a problem because of me.

I nodded at her then took my phone from her as it rang. When I saw Jessica's number, I knew she'd talked to Decaurey. I wasn't ready to have that conversation with her. She was another one that could get me all fired up for no reason. Whenever I was having moments of mania, I didn't talk to her. I knew that I should have made her aware of my condition, but once again, I was embarrassed about it.

So many people were revealing their truths though. People seemed to be more accepting of mental illnesses and tried to understand it. I would be taking a risk by telling her, because I didn't know if she would be one of those people. I loved Jess, and I couldn't lose her friendship. She gave great advice, and I tried to return the favor. When I was stable mentally, I found that I gave really great advice as well.

After declining her call, I called Shylou. He answered, sounding upbeat as hell. "What it do, baby girl?"

I smiled slightly. "Hey, Shylou. What's up?"

"You know what's up. What's going on with you? Carter told me Decaurey had asked questions about you and if we'd witnessed your mood swings. I really don't want to tell him your business, but I think *you* need to."

"I can't."

"Why?"

"He's going to look at me differently."

"Ty, really? That nigga already looking at you differently. He trying to figure out where the woman at that he talked to for three months. If he weren't trying to figure you out, then that would mean he didn't give a fuck. He's trying to find an excuse for your behavior. What does that say to you, baby? What do you have to lose by telling him? I mean, if you're pushing him away, you still don't have him. At least he'll know why. You owe him an explanation, if nothing more."

I took a deep breath and couldn't stop the tears from falling down my cheeks. "I had a bout of insomnia. I was so damned tired, but I couldn't fall asleep. It was extremely hard to stay in pocket. However, during sex, it's like I can't control it. It seems like that's when he sees me at my best and my worst simultaneously."

"And that's more of a reason you need to tell him what's up. At that moment, you should be more 'in pocket' than ever," he said, enunciating in pocket.

I could imagine he'd probably held up his fingers to do air quotes. I remained quiet, trying to make sense of what he was saying. My baby sat next to me and wiped my cheeks then kissed me. "I have to think about it, Shy. I probably won't ever be able to be around the family again if he's telling people something is wrong with me."

"I don't think he's mentioned it to anyone other than Carter and Jess. Those are the two people he has access to that know you better than he does. Plus, the only Henderson that don't let shit go at times is Storm." He chuckled. "You wouldn't believe me though if I told you he and W.J. got into it several times. You can't even tell there used to be a rift between them."

"Yeah, but that's his brother. I'm an outsider, Shy."

"No, you aren't. You're like a sister to Jess. That makes you family. I'm a friend of Kenny's. That was how I became family. Family may have arguments and get angry with one another, but most importantly, they love each other and just want what's best for each other... at least the Hendersons do. Some families are full of hate and malice. That's not them. You've met them at their best. Capitalize off that. Whether you realize it or not, you have family in us."

I only cried more, and this time, it was audible. I could no longer contain it. "Damn, Ty. Don't cry, baby girl. Do I need to get Cass on the phone to fire you back up?"

"Shy, shut the fuck up!" Cass yelled in the background as he chuckled.

I chuckled through my tears and audible cries. How bipolar was that shit? When I calmed down, I said, "You're right. I appreciate y'all so much. You always look out for me. God put you in my life for that very reason. Thank you, Shy. I'm going to try to make this right."

"A'ight. You know if you ever need us, we're always here. Get you some rest and start fresh in the morning. Don't call anyone tonight."

"You're right. I need to sleep. I'll call Jess when we get on the road. I need to talk to Decaurey in person."

"Umm... you may wanna call him first too. Given his mindset right now, he may not want to see you."

I lowered my head, wanting to cry all over again, but I refused to do so. "If I tell him I'm ready to talk, he won't mind seeing me."

"Okay. Well go to bed. Holla at me later."

"I will. Good night, and thanks again."

I ended the call as Angel gave me a tight-lipped smile. "Did he sound angry when you spoke to him?"

"No. He sounded relieved."

I nodded as she gently rubbed circles on my back. "Okay, baby.

Let's get some rest. I want to get on the road early tomorrow morning."

"Okay."

She got up and went to her bed as I lay on my side, my back to her. Jess had sent a text. I just knew she would be cursing me out, but like Shylou had said, I found the opposite.

*Ty, I'm worried about you, boo. Please call me when you can. Love you.*

I closed my eyes after I set my phone on the nightstand. I had to make things right. Once I prayed silently, I drifted off to sleep.

---

WE'D BEEN on the road for two, almost three hours, and it was only nine in the morning. I stopped to get coffee and for Angel to get something to eat. Neither of us could stand to eat first thing in the morning so we'd waited until now. Our stomachs got angry if we did. Thankfully, I'd been finding pull-through parking to where I didn't have to back this trailer up too much, because that shit was a task. Trying to remember to turn the wheel the opposite direction I wanted the trailer to go was tiring.

Once we got back in the Tahoe, I grabbed my phone and took a deep breath, preparing to call Jess. I glanced over at my daughter, and she was eating a whole ass corn dog and had some type of chicken and cheese taquito that had my stomach cutting flips at the sight of it. I hit her name in my missed calls log, and she answered on the first ring.

"Ty! Thank God. Girl, I was so worried. You good?"

"Hey, Jess. I'm okay. I needed to get some much-needed rest before I returned your call. I'd been awake for nearly forty-eight hours."

"Damn. That insomnia came back with a vengeance, huh?"

"Hell yeah. I umm... I owe you and Decaurey an explanation for my behavior."

"Girl, you don't owe me shit. You may owe him though. I'm just glad you're okay. However, if you want to explain to me what's going on with you, I'm going to listen and do my best to help you if I can."

My body heated up with love as I listened to my friend express how much I meant to her. I couldn't stop the smile that appeared on my face. When I got ready to speak again, it fell from my lips. There was nothing heartwarming about what I was about to tell her. "Jess, I get insomnia from time to time because of the medication I'm on. It's supposed to be helping with depression and other things, but insomnia is one of the side effects."

She was quiet for a moment. "Well, that's some backwards ass shit. How the fuck you supposed to *not* be depressed when you can't fucking sleep?"

I chuckled. She was right as hell. It was the same mindset I had whenever I decided to forgo taking it. She grabbed my attention again when she asked, "What other things are you taking the medicine for?"

"Anxiety. But more importantly, Jess, to control my manic episodes. I have bipolar disorder."

She was quiet for a moment as my heart rate increased, and sweat started to accumulate in my brow. "That's it?"

I frowned. "What do you mean, that's it?"

"Shit, I thought you were about to tell me something heavier than that. Not making light of your mental state at all, but sometimes I think a lot of people go undiagnosed. I think it's more common than you realize. But sis, you killing it! You aren't letting that shit define who you are."

I smiled slightly. "So it doesn't change the way you see me?"

"Hell no! If anything, I can understand you better. I'm glad you told me. When are you going to tell Decaurey?"

"I wanna tell him face to face when I come to get my car. Shylou said he has to go out there to handle some business with Kenny, so he'll make sure I get to Beaumont. Where are you?"

"Heading to the airport. I have a shoot in Brazil, baby!"

"Lucky ass. I haven't been to Brazil in a hot ass minute. Who you out there for? Shy or Carter?"

"Shy."

"Wait 'til I see his ass later."

She laughed and I did too. It felt so freeing to tell her what the deal was with me. As we remained quiet, soaking in the silence, Jess said, "He just wants to love on you, Ty. He's a peaceful guy, but because he doesn't know what's going on with you, he's trying to be done. Don't take too long to talk to him. He was so angry when he got to Nome. I could still see how hurt and worried he was through his frowns and aggressive talk though. You are the first girlfriend he's had in over seven years."

"I know. I won't wait too long. I plan to talk to him today, but if he's not home, I'll call him. If he doesn't answer, I'll send a long ass text. He deserves to know, even if we don't get back together."

"Y'all were a couple?"

"Yeah, no matter how short that time was. I told him I was his night before last, after three months of talking and getting to know one another. Well... me getting to know him, because I was guarded and keeping shit from him."

"Damn. So how long before y'all get to Houston?"

"A little over six hours."

"Okay. I'm almost to the airport, so I will call you back once I get to my gate."

"Okay. Talk to you then."

I ended the call and glanced at Angel to see she was knocked the hell out. I chuckled. Some kind of road dawg she was. I decided to go ahead and text Decaurey. That way if he wasn't home, I would know it was because he didn't want to see me. After taking a deep breath, I pulled over for a moment. Since I needed to focus on how I would word this message, I knew it was best that I pulled over.

*Hi, Decaurey. I'm so sorry about my behavior. I want to talk to you about it when I get to your place to get my car. I don't think it's something I should send in a text unless I don't have a choice. I owe you an explanation. I fucked things up between us, and I need to make them right, even if you choose not to pursue a relationship with me. Text me back and let me know what you decide.*

After I turned on some Teddy Pendergrass, I got back on the road. My daddy loved Teddy P. Sometimes I thought that nigga thought he was him. Whenever I looked back at old pictures of us, he seemed to dress just like him. I laughed every time I looked at them. "Love TKO" was playing through the speakers, and I couldn't help but let my thoughts go back to Decaurey. We weren't in love, but that shit I put him through had knocked him far away from it like a one-two punch.

He still hadn't responded, and I could only hope that he would… either way.

## CHAPTER NINE

### DECAUREY

I huffed as I made my way inside the bank. To say it was damn near October, it was still hot as hell outside. It wasn't in the hundreds like it was in August, but shit, the nineties weren't that much better. One of my customers paid ten grand in cash for a job, so I knew I had to go to the bank with that. I hated carrying that much cash around. A nigga was asking to get robbed. Plus, other niggas that worked for me seemed to be a little unsavory at times. My best bet was to keep an honest thief honest.

I wasn't about to leave shit sitting around to tempt them with. They were the type of niggas that wouldn't break in yo' shit, but if you left the door unlocked, they might go through it. That was what people referred to as an honest thief. It was contradictory as hell, but I understood it well.

After making my deposit, I went back to my work truck and just sat there soaking up the cool air. Before I went in, I read a text from Tyeis. Her message had me irritated as fuck. It was like when her name flashed across the screen, I saw red. She finally wanted to talk, although she had plenty of opportunity to talk. I asked her what was up with her more than a few times. The only thing she came up with was depression.

I was still too angry to talk to her face to face. I didn't want to see her right now. She made me weak. Her presence would have me forgetting about everything and fucking her pussy out the frame. I had to stand my ground, and truth was, I needed time to get over this shit. She literally left me in another fucking state. If I were in the financial predicament I was in ten years ago, my ass would have practically been stranded.

I was happy that Angel and I had exchanged numbers. She called me last night to let me know they were safe. She'd also said she would text me to let me know when they made it safely to Houston. Had it not been for her, I wouldn't have known a thing. I finally pulled out of the parking lot and prepared to head to the diner. It was Tuesday, and I had to go get those smothered pork chops. Everyone raved about Aunt Jen's stuffed fried chicken, and it was good as hell, but those smothered pork chops that Aunt Chrissy did were my weakness.

Every Tuesday, my inner fat boy was excited as hell. I'd get the smothered pork chops, rice, gravy, cornbread, greens, and macaroni and cheese or potato salad. Today I was more in the mood for the mac and cheese, so hopefully that was what they chose since they had potato salad last week. All the Hendersons knew where to find me at lunchtime on Tuesdays. My fixation with the Henderson sisters' cooking was no secret to nobody. I used to go damn near every day. I was down to twice a week now, Tuesdays and Fridays.

On Fridays, most of the family would be there at lunchtime until they closed. They only stayed open late one night during the week for family night, and that was on Thursdays. As I continued to drive, my phone rang. It was one of my guys. They were in Beaumont working on the cement pad for a new apartment complex. Hopefully, all was well, because I wasn't trying to miss my pork chops. "Hello?"

"What's up, boss? I was calling because Greg went home sick. Nigga was throwing up everywhere."

*Fuck!* "A'ight. I'm gon' head back that way."

"No need. We got it. I just wanted to let you know."

Shiiid, fat boy was happier than that nigga on *First Sunday* blowing that damn bugle. "You sure?"

"Yep. If we need anything before you come back, I'll holla."

"A'ight, man. Thanks."

I ended the call and checked the text message that had come through while I was on the phone. *Storm Henderson.* I slightly rolled my eyes. He was always texting me with bullshit. The election was coming up in a month and a half, and that nigga was working everybody's nerves. I checked it while I was at the traffic light in China to see what he had to say. *You coming to headquarters today?*

I chuckled and shook my head. *I'm on my way to the diner for lunch.*

*Nigga, I already owe you for your fucked up comment from yesterday. See you when you get here.*

This nigga was gonna be the death of me. I was only five minutes away, if that. On a good day, I could make it in three. When I got there, his tall ass was standing outside talking to some white man with a frown on his face. *Aww shit.* I thought I was tall at six two until I met these Henderson brothers. The shortest one was my height. Storm was the tallest. Nobody around here was under six feet. I believed Malachi was the shortest. He was six feet even.

I got out of my truck, and he glanced my way, then waved me over. I didn't recognize the gentleman he was talking to, so I hoped this shit was on the up and up. When I walked up on them, he slapped my hand and turned back to the man. "Darren, this is my nephew, Decaurey. He owns Franklin Cement Finishers. Now like I said, we don't need your services. We got Nome sewed up. No need in coming out here soliciting. If we need you, we'll call."

When the man walked away with a red face, Storm said under his breath, "Na get the fuck on."

I chuckled as he said, "They think it ain't nothing but a bunch of country bumpkins out here that don't know shit. Had I not been mayor, I would've cussed his ass out."

"You ain't mayor though."

He side-eyed me then swiftly looped his arm around my head and put me in a headlock. I swore he thought I was a kid. "Nigga, save this shit for your bad ass sons."

He laughed and pushed me away from him as Jasper drove up. "See, I was gonna ask you about pouring cement at the shop for a new mechanic bay, but I may need to call ol' boy back."

"Whatever. You expanding? That's what's up."

"Yep. Lots of black people are moving to the area thanks to Nesha's village out there. It's giving all of us more business, even Marcus. They eating those custom rims up! We just need a couple of doctors and a dentist."

"Hell yeah. Any prospects?"

"Mm hmm. Maui wants to be a dentist. The twins plan to go to school to be a gynecologist and an obstetrician. They plan to open a practice together right out here. Before you know it, we gon' have a whole fucking hospital."

"Hell yeah."

"What's up, y'all?" Jasper said as he approached and slapped both our hands.

We headed inside, and when Jakari saw us, he stood and came to greet us as well. We all sat at the table with him, Philly, and Pop. Uncle Kenny came in right after us. Once we were all seated, Aunt Chrissy and Aunt Jen came and greeted us, then went back to the kitchen to fix everyone's plates. They knew what we all wanted without even asking.

"What's up, son?" Pop said.

"Too much and nothing at the same time."

"I got some more business for you. We're adding on to the family barn since the family has been expanding. We need more room."

"That's what's up. Y'all need to go on and hire me to permanently be a part of the family business."

They all glanced at each other. "You mean like buy out your business?" Kenny asked.

"I mean put me on lock to where I don't have time to accept work from outsiders. I can work exclusively for Henderson Ranch and Farms."

"Actually, I was going to bring that up in the meeting this evening," Pop said.

My eyebrows lifted. I was shocked. I was just fucking with them. Before I could say anything, Brix and Marcus joined us. "Yo, when Jess get back, it will be time for the photo shoot with Noooooah!" Jasper said. "You ready?"

We all chuckled at the way he said Noah's name. Everyone in the entertainment industry said his name that way. "Yeah, man. I'm ready. He requested that I let the grass grow out a bit, so I haven't cut in two weeks."

"That's what's up. Jess ready?"

"Yeah. She seems a little nervous though. This is her first big gig."

Everyone knew that Nate was the reason she'd gotten that job, and we could all see how uncomfortable Brix seemed. Pop changed the subject and asked, "How's the gym doing?"

"It's doing great, Uncle W.J. Thanks. It helps that all of you have memberships," Brix responded and chuckled.

Despite how smooth Pop was with the change of subject, it didn't stop everyone from noticing Brix's demeanor change with the subject. Storm was frowning, so I knew some slick shit was about to fall out of his mouth. "If Jess wanted him, she would be with him," he said, not letting me down.

"I know that. It ain't her I'm worried about."

"That nigga would be a fool to come out here and start some shit," Kenny added.

"I'm not saying he would even start shit. Just knowing he's seen every part of her that I've seen bothers me. It only bothers me because I know they still talk occasionally. Before you ask, she told me and showed me their thread. It dated back all the way when she and I had first worked things out. None of the conversation was inappropriate. But I told her that I wasn't feeling it one bit, no matter how much she trusted him to be respectful. She told me she would pass the word on to him and that she was more than sure he would understand."

That situation was tough as hell. However, I was grateful for their drama because it took my mind off mine. No one added to what he said because Aunt Chrissy and Aunt Jen had begun setting plates in front of everybody. All conversation had to cease because I'd be damned if my pork chops with that sixty-weight gravy was gonna get cold.

As I began eating, my phone chimed with a text. For some reason, I felt in my heart that it was Tyeis. I never responded to her message earlier. That was a little over an hour ago that she'd sent it. I pulled my phone from my pocket to confirm my suspicion. I was right. *Okay, I suppose you don't want to see me. Maybe we can have a phone conversation then. Can I call you in a couple of hours?*

I checked the time to see that it was nearly eleven thirty. I needed time to think. I was petty as fuck, and my mind kept saying, *she's on your time now. When you wanted her to talk to you, she had nothing to say.* After taking a deep breath, against my better judgment, I responded. *Yeah.*

That meant she would be calling me around one thirty. I should be long gone from this place by then. "What got you looking all sour all of a sudden?" Marcus asked.

"Probably Tyeis. That nigga don't know whether he coming or going. She got him all sprung and shit," Storm said.

"Man, shut up," I said. "Find you some business besides mine."

He frowned like that was supposed to scare me. Before he could say something else, Jasper interrupted and said, "Leave that man alone. Remember when Aspen had you all scared she was gon' leave yo' ass? You didn't wanna talk to nobody either," Jasper said.

"Nigga, ain't nobody talking about me."

I slowly shook my head as I went to the front to get a box. Pop joined me at the counter. "Don't pay Storm no attention."

"I'm not. It's not him that I'm actually irritated with. He was just the perfect person to lash out at. He's right though. Tyeis is on my last fucking nerve. She left me in D.C. I had to catch a flight back. That's why I'm back so early. I should still be on the road right now. I don't know how I overslept, but I did. When I woke up, her ass was in the wind. I don't need that kind of drama in my life. She finally wants to talk about what's up with her, but I'd been asking her for the past three days and she kept saying nothing."

"How you feel about her though? It seems like you care a lot for her."

"I do, but I don't wanna deal with no bullshit. That's why I'm so angry about it. I feel like she wasting my time. I'm ready for a meaningful relationship. I've spent almost the past seven years getting myself together so I can be ready for whenever it came along. I feel like she was a damn smoke screen."

"Are you going to at least talk to her and see what she has to say?"

"Yeah. She's gonna call in a couple of hours."

"I hope it works out for the best."

I nodded, then grabbed a box and headed back to box my food up. Jakari was watching me extra hard though. "Man, quit staring at me before you make me drop my food."

"Aww, nigga, Mama will fix you another plate."

Aunt Chrissy was his mama. "Don't mean I wanna drop this one." I glanced over at Storm and said, "I apologize, Uncle Mayor. You right. She got me fucked up."

He smirked. "I see you taking a page from Jessica's book by calling me Uncle Mayor. Smart move. I can be buttered up, especially with that."

I chuckled then shook everyone's hands. When I got to Jasper, I reminded him of my appointment tomorrow to get my hair cut and beard trimmed. The minute I walked outside, Nesha was walking in. "You late, sis. You was busy?"

"Yeah. I was drawing up your contract."

She winked at me and kissed my cheek then headed inside as I went to my truck. I knew they had been waiting for me to get more established and get more practice in with everyone else before having me work on anything for the business. They all had me doing their personal shit and for their personal businesses, but to have Henderson Ranch and Farms in my bag was a huge accomplishment. I'd worked hard for something like that. With the way the business was growing, I knew they would keep me busy.

## CHAPTER TEN

### TYEIS

I was nervous as hell. It was one thirty, and it was time to call Decaurey. I hated that he didn't want to see me, but I supposed I understood. I was just happy he was allowing me to even explain. He could have told me to go to hell. I glanced over at Angel, and she gave me a reassuring smile. "You got this," she said as she rubbed my arm.

I clicked his name from one of his many calls and waited for him to answer. My hand was trembling, and I could feel the perspiration accumulating under my breasts. By the third ring I was about to end the call, but he answered. "Hello?"

"Hi, Decaurey."

"What's up?" he asked, sounding completely nonchalant.

"How was your flight?" I asked, then immediately regretted it.

"Tyeis, if you wanna talk, talk. I'm not up for casual conversation like you aren't the reason I was on a flight back to begin with."

I took a deep, shaky breath. "I know you're tired of my apologies without explanation. However, I'm going to apologize again first. I'm apologizing for my mood swings and spotty behavior. I apologize for lying to you. You asked if the only thing going on with me was depression, and I said yes. That wasn't the truth."

I was so fucking scared to tell him. It was like my tongue locked in place as I stared at the passing scenery. We were nearly in Beaumont, and I just wished he would have agreed to see me. Finally, he asked, "What's the truth then? I gotta get back to work."

"I... uh..."

I was stuttering bad. Angel grabbed my hand as I struggled to get it out. "Go 'head, Mama," she encouraged.

"The other night, I was moody, cranky, and irritable because I was dealing with a bout of insomnia. The other medication I'm on can cause that at times. Decaurey, I have bipolar disorder. It triggers my anxiety and depression. The medications I'm on are supposed to help with that, and for the most part, they do... when I take them. Sometimes I don't take them, especially when I'm dealing with insomnia. Before last night, I had been awake for forty-eight hours. That's when you get the Tyeis you saw night before last."

"So, just leave me in D.C. because you were tired and irritable."

"Decaurey, my decisions can be fucked up sometimes. That was a horrible decision."

"Why didn't you tell me?"

"I was scared you wouldn't want to deal with it and that you would leave me. I wanted you to get to know me better before I told you. I wouldn't be telling you now had it not been for what happened."

"Well, you not telling me had the same effect. I don't give a fuck about your illness, Tyeis. I could have handled the situation a lot better had I known. I can't stand a liar though. I don't like being deceived. That's what this feels like. You should have been straightforward with me. I have to go."

"Decaurey! Wait!"

"Man, what?"

"I'm so sorry. Please forgive me. I'm trying to make things right with you. Hearing this angry side of you hurts like you wouldn't believe."

"Good. Now you know how I felt yesterday morning when I woke up and you were gone. Bye, Tyeis."

He ended the call, and I felt like I was hyperventilating. My fear had destroyed my future, and I didn't know how I would handle knowing that. Angel was still rubbing my arm, doing her best to console me as I drove. I said that I would have to be okay with him not wanting to be in a relationship with me anymore, but now that I'd experienced his rejection, it hurt. I knew he was hurt by my actions, but I supposed I was hoping my revelation would soften his heart again.

I was so wrong. I could hear his hurt and anger in every word he spoke. Now I knew why he didn't want to see me. My actions had hurt him so badly he couldn't or didn't want to handle the sight of me. The tears fell, despite me trying to hold them in. I quickly swiped them away as I exited the freeway. "You want something to eat? There's a Jack-in-the-Box, McDonald's, and I think a wing place close."

"Oooh, wings!" she said with a smile.

I gave her a slight smile and made my way to the place I knew of. I couldn't remember the name of it until I got there. *Kickin' Chicken.* Jess swore by this place whenever we came to Beaumont for anything. I made the block and parked on the side street so I wouldn't have to back up, and we walked to the restaurant.

I didn't know how I would keep it together on the way home. I always took Highway 90 to get to Houston, and that meant I would have to pass right through Nome. While Decaurey didn't live in Nome, he spent a lot of time there, because that was where his family was. I could only pray that I would get a glimpse of him. It wasn't like I could stop to see Jess. She was on her way to Brazil. She'd called an hour ago to say they had boarded and would call me when she landed. That would be around ten tonight.

After we placed our orders, we sat at a table to wait. Angel was playing a game on her phone, and I decided to scroll social media. Seeing all the posts about happiness and success were irritating me, because my life was in shambles. It was all my fault. I didn't take my medicine again this morning, but I told myself that once we got Angel's things in storage and her personal items home, my sabbatical could end. I would take them in the morning hopefully. I couldn't risk not being able to sleep tonight.

Monday, I would be flying out to New York for a shoot for Nordstrom. I was surprised I had to go to New York instead of doing it right there in H-Town. I wasn't complaining about it though. I could use time away from everything. I would be making a quick turnaround. Wednesday evening next week, I would be back home. The shoot was Tuesday.

Once the lady brought out our food, I set my phone on the table and dug into my lemon pepper wings. I hadn't had wings in a hot minute, and I didn't know why with as much as I loved them. That was one thing I missed about working in the office. Shylou was always introducing us to new foods and new restaurants in Houston. There was only about twelve of us in his administrative office, so we benefitted quite a bit. He was able to buy food without it costing him an arm and a leg. Every Friday, we knew to expect something delicious and filling.

I would probably go into the office Friday just to see how things were going. Sometimes the HR director had shit she needed help with. I surely wasn't going just to visit. It was all about my money. Shylou compensated me whenever I went in. I didn't really like any of those bitches in the office. They didn't like me either. The difference between them and me was that I didn't give a fuck. It was like Shylou attracted the hood ratchet of Houston. His clothing stores catered to them at first, so whenever they saw a now hiring sign, it was open season.

It didn't help that Shylou liked that hood shit at times. I noticed that with Cass. He liked getting her all worked up so he could laugh. He was an entire nut. It surprised me that he was so business savvy because I'd seen his hood side first at a comedy show in Houston years ago. He was a nice-looking man, and the women didn't mind telling him. When I applied for a job at his business office from an ad on Indeed, I was shocked to see he was the one interviewing me.

When I met his business side, I was thoroughly impressed and accepted the job on the spot. After seeing I was a college graduate and that I had a couple of years of experience in human resources, he offered me the job immediately. We got close, and I was grateful for his friendship. From his friendship, I gained Cass as a friend as well. She loved the fact that I wasn't like those hoes in the office. She'd told me about her issues with them when she first moved to town and became the office manager.

Once we were done eating, we headed back to the truck. On our way, Angel said, "Mama, I think Decaurey is going to come around. He's just angry right now."

I glanced at her. "You think so?"

"Yes. I think he likes you a lot and that your illness doesn't matter to him. Neither does mine. Umm… when we get in the vehicle, I have something to tell you."

I didn't know if I could take any more bad news today, but I turned to her and said, "Okay."

Before I could even take off good, she said, "I got a phone call while I was in D.C. from bitch ass Kelvin."

I shoved the SUV back in park and turned to her, my eyes wide. "What the fuck did he want? And how did he get your number?"

Just the fact that she called him bitch ass Kelvin like I did, put me on high alert. She never referred to him as that because she said she didn't know him to call him such things. She refused to talk down on anybody unless she had a personal experience with them, no matter how much I didn't like them. I supposed that was a good attribute to have. So apparently, her encounter with him wasn't a good one.

"I met a guy at school that was really cool, and he'd asked me for my number because he said he could see I was pretty good with college algebra, and he would need a tutor. We met at the library not long after and he'd asked where I was from. I told him that I was born in Houston, but my mama had roots in Columbia, South Carolina. We kept talking, and I found out that he was my brother."

"Brother!" I yelled, probably looking like Soulja Boy at the Breakfast Club interview.

"Yeah. He asked if he could give his dad my phone number, and I said yes. He said his dad had mentioned me, telling him that he had a sister out there somewhere."

"That jackass! My number hasn't changed. If he wanted to get acquainted, he could have made arrangements. We all grow up and change. I would have given him a chance to make it right!"

"Well, he called later that night. He introduced himself and said he was glad to make my acquaintance, but the conversation went downhill when he said he thought down syndrome would have had me looking like those kids on TV and that he wouldn't be able to effectively communicate with me because of it. I kind of let that pass. He asked for a picture, and when I sent it to him, he said, *Oh yeah. I can tell you have down syndrome by the way you look.* He's an insensitive ass. After that, I said, *Bye, bitch ass Kelvin* and ended the call in his face."

I couldn't believe she had been subjected to that shit. I wanted to find his ass when we got back and fuck his world up. My chest was rising and falling rapidly as I tried to calm myself down. "What did his son say when you saw him again? What's his name?"

"He apologized for him. His name is Creed."

"Creed?"

"Yeah. His mama is a fan of Michael B. Jordan, and she literally had his name changed when he was ten years old when the movie Creed came out."

"What kind of fucked up shit is that?"

Angel giggled. "I thought the same thing. He's nice though. When I told him I was leaving, he begged me to keep in touch. He wanted to meet you, but I told him I didn't think it was a good idea. I didn't want you to take the bad stuff his dad did out on him."

"You think I'm that shallow and petty, Angel?" I asked, barely able to hold in my laughter.

She just stared at me, which pulled the laugh right out of me. I needed this laughter. Once I calmed down, I said, "I'm sorry you had a fucked-up experience with bitch ass Kelvin."

"You said he left because of your illness, but he left because of mine, didn't he?"

I took a deep breath. I never wanted her to feel like anything was her fault. "Baby, that doesn't matter. He's a fucked-up individual that can only hand out fucked up experiences. I never wanted you to think that him leaving was your fault. Now that you're older, I think you can understand that. I just wish I would have seen that side of him a long time ago, before I got pregnant. I could've attracted someone better to where you would have had a loving father. I truly wish your dad was someone else... someone you could look up to and respect."

"Decaurey could be my dad. I think he would love the title," she said as her phone chimed.

I lowered my head. She just had to mention Decaurey. I knew she didn't understand just how much this was hurting me. Whenever she got angry, she was never angry long, and I believed she thought I was wired the same way. "Who messaged you?" I asked softly.

"Creed," she said, then giggled.

I couldn't help but giggle, too, as I made my way back to the interstate. From my peripheral, I could see her replying to his text. As if reading my mind, she said, "He was checking to see if we'd made it back to Houston. We're like almost two hours away?"

"Yeah. Like an hour and a half."

She nodded and went back to her phone. I couldn't stop my mind from wandering back to Decaurey. I didn't want to go against his wishes, but I didn't want to give up on us either. He never really said that he would never consider being with me again. He *did* say that he couldn't stand liars, but he only knew I lied because I admitted it. I grabbed my phone as we exited College Street. College Street in Beaumont turned into Highway 90 once outside of the city limits.

Once I got to the traffic light at 23rd Street, I sent him a text. *I can't give up on us. I still have hope that we are meant to be. You didn't say you no longer saw me in your future. While I know you may need time away from me, I'm not going to disappear. I get it because sometimes even I need time away from me. I like you a lot, Decaurey, and I know you like me a lot too. I won't bombard you with messages, but always know that I'll always be thinking about you and trying to find ways to obtain your heart.*

The car blowing their horn behind me got my attention. I took off from the light as I hit send, hoping he hadn't blocked me by now. I didn't expect him to respond to my message, but I hoped he would at least read it and feel how serious I was. I wouldn't rest until he was mine again, even if I had to be like the music group Jade and beg him not to walk away.

## CHAPTER ELEVEN

### DECAUREY

"It's too hot to be dealing with fucking cement. What made you want to get into this business anyway?" Jakari asked me.

"I worked with one of my mama's cousins during the summers, and for some reason, I took a liking to it."

He'd gotten in the truck with me as I headed to the post office. I'd gotten a post office box in Nome since I would be moving here soon. I sent all my mail to this address. Mostly everything was paperless, but for the shit that wasn't, it came here. We walked inside, and Kathleen greeted us then went to the back. I used my key to check my box, and nothing was in there.

As we headed to the counter for him to send certified documents to someone for the business, Kathleen came back with a box. "Decaurey, this came for you today."

I frowned slightly. I wasn't expecting anything, and there was no return address on it. "Hmm. Okay. Thanks."

I headed to the truck as Jakari handled his business and used my key to cut the tape off the box. When I opened it and saw the brand-new Stetson, I knew where it had come from. *Tyeis*. It had been almost two weeks since I'd spoken to her. My conscience ate me alive the day I hung up on her. I was so angry and hurt. Then I never responded to her text about her not giving up.

She sent me a belt buckle early last week. The shit was blinged out and looked like something I would wear to a trail ride. She knew how much I enjoyed the country and turning up at a trail ride party. I lived for the shit. I'd returned it to her only for her to send it back. If she wanted to spend her money on me, then she could have at it. I wasn't sending this Stetson back. It was a felt one too. I couldn't wait for the winter to roll around so I could wear it.

When Jakari got inside the truck, his eyebrows lifted, and he whistled. "That's a nice ass hat. Don't tell me. Tyeis bought it."

"Yep. I ain't sending this shit back though."

Jakari laughed as I put it back in the box it came in and set it on the back seat. "So you going to the shoot tomorrow?" he asked.

"Hell yeah. I wouldn't miss it for the world. I'm sure everybody's gonna be out there."

"Yep. Aunt Tiff and her relay team is going to be out there too. The video and song are about him falling in love with a country girl. Jess gon' eat that shit up."

"Oh, I know. Any word on the situation with Nate?" I asked.

"I think he's here."

"Aww shit. Well, hopefully, he keeps his eyeballs where they belong. I would hate for Brix to get ahold of him. That would be like a Pitbull attacking a Chihuahua."

Jakari laughed. "I don't like how you making Nate out to be weak and shit."

"I'm not saying he's weak, but I don't think he's a match for Brixton. He just seem way too friendly."

Jakari shook his head as I pulled out of the parking lot and headed back to the Henderson business office. "That's the ones that'll surprise you though. Friendly people and gay men. They'll whup yo' ass!"

I laughed hard as I turned on Highway 326. "Nigga, you ain't lying! You ever seen a gay man fight? I ain't talking about on TV neither."

"Just on TV, man," he said.

"Shiiiid, I'll never forget it. He had my respect that day."

We laughed more as I turned into the lot of the office. Once he got out, promising to hook up later, I headed back to the job site to see how things were going. There was no way I would leave them unsupervised without checking in for too long since they were working on my people's shit. It needed to be right from jump. There was no room for error.

As I parked at Storm's shop, I couldn't help but allow my mind to travel back to Tyeis. She would probably be here tomorrow if she didn't have a job scheduled. I grabbed my phone to send her a thank you message, but then put the phone down. I knew if I texted her, she would take it as I was ready to get back with her. I wasn't ready for that, and I didn't know if I ever would be. The last thing I wanted to do was give her false hope.

When I made up my mind about whether I wanted to pursue something with her again or not, then I would reach out to her, not a moment sooner. I didn't know how I would avoid her, though, if she showed up out here tomorrow. I wouldn't be able to focus on Nate and Brix if I was watching her ass. Angel had texted me a few times to see if I'd had a chance to get into *Hunter X Hunter* yet, but I hadn't even thought about that shit since all this had gone down with Tyeis.

Since I'd watched the season finale of *Demon Slayer,* I hadn't even thought about Anime. The season wouldn't come back on until next year. I told her that when I had time, I would watch the new-to-me show. I hated that I couldn't really invest time into getting to know her. There was no way I could form a bond with Angel without being with Tyeis. I didn't want to hurt Angel though. So whenever she texted me, I responded, asking how she and her mother were doing.

The knock on my window scared the fuck out of me. When I saw

Storm's face, I rolled my eyes. That was a common occurrence whenever I was around his ass. I rolled the window down as a smirk appeared on his lips. "What'chu sitting out here for? They ain't gon' mess up. They know who this shit belong to."

"Well, I wanna be sure they don't. That cool wit'chu?"

"Whatever float yo' boat."

"You about to go home for the day?" I asked.

"Yeah. Aspen said Remy giving her the blues today. I gotta go tighten his lil ass up."

I chuckled. "The twins are in their senior year of school, right?"

"Yeah. I'm ready to shove their asses out the door too. They both already have scholarships to Spellman."

"That's good though. At least they're smart."

"They didn't have a choice. You see who their parents are?" He chuckled. "Naw, that's my babies. They always got my back, no matter what. I can be wrong as hell, which is seldom, by the way, but they gon' be ten toes down for a nigga. After the fact, they'll tell me how wrong I was, but they just gon' be wrong with me to help me get my point across."

I laughed. "That's riders for real though."

"So what's up wit' chu and Jess's friend?"

"Nothing."

"That's all I get? No details?"

I side-eyed him. Storm was the kind of nigga that would throw shit back in your face and have you ready to fight his ass. "Man, you know how you are. I would be a fool to give yo' ass ammunition to use against me."

He chuckled and slid his hand over his beard. "A'ight, a'ight. But listen. If you thinking about her every day, then you might as well see if it can be fixed. You gon' be miserable until you do."

With that, he walked off. *Well, I'll be damn.* Storm was finally giving advice that made sense.

# DON'T WALK AWAY

WHEN I GOT to Brixton's stables, there were a ton of cars out there. People were everywhere, and the sheriff's department had shit blocked off. People on Highway 365 were being rerouted through the neighborhood. I knew those white people were pissed about that. The thought of the complaints made me chuckle. The killing part was that the complaints were getting handled by Storm and Marcus.

Storm was still the mayor pro tem since Abney never came back. I wouldn't be surprised if their asses told those people to go fuck themselves. It wasn't like there was a whole lot of traffic on the weekends anyway. Now if it were a weekday, I would be a little salty about that shit too. Nobody wanted a bunch of traffic being rerouted through their neighborhoods.

When I got out of the truck, I made my way to the barricade where someone was standing with a clipboard. "What's your name, sir?"

"Decaurey Franklin."

After she found my name, she nodded at the officer, and he let me through. I was a little late because my nerves were getting the best of me. I wore my straw Stetson since it was still warm outside and the belt buckle Tyeis bought me. They'd asked everyone to be in country attire, but authentic attire... not that over-the-top shit city folks did when they were trying to look the part. That shit on social media wasn't how real country folk did it. Now, we did look fly, but that was excessive, especially for the men.

We'd all had a good laugh about that shit. It looked good to other people and got them the attention they were looking for, but we knew better. When I walked through the area, I saw Aunt Tiff and her team on horses. When I saw Pop and my mama, I made my way to them. I sat next to her and kissed her cheek. "What's up, Ma?"

"Hey, baby. How was your day?"

"It was— whoa! Aunt Jen and Aunt Chrissy cooking?"

95

Pop laughed and slowly shook his head. "How do you know it's them?"

"As much as I eat there? I could smell that in Alaska and would know it was them, so I would surely know it was their cooking right here at home."

He laughed. "Yeah. They wanted Noah to have some authentic southern cooking. They rented a food truck and got it cracking. I told them they ought to just buy one. There were too many events going on in Beaumont this summer that they could have been a part of had they had it. So they said they would think about it and see if it would fit in their budget for next year."

"That's what's up. What are they cooking?"

"You know Jen is doing the stuffed fried chicken. I think Chrissy is doing beef tips and pork chops too. There's no limit on the sides. I believe they are also doing a court bouillon at Noah's request. They are cooking a feast."

"Hell yeah," I said as I saw Jakari and Nate walk toward us.

I slowly shook my head. I didn't know if Nate was tripping or what. He and Noah considered themselves brothers now, so that was probably why he was here. Basketball season was about to get cranked up in a little bit, so I was hoping he wouldn't show up. I stood from my seat and shook his hand. "What's up, man?"

"What's up? How you been?"

"Good."

He and Jakari took a seat by us for a moment and continued talking. Then I heard him ask, "Is that Jessica's fiancé?"

I looked in the direction his gaze was trained and said, "Yeah, that's him."

He nodded. "I'm gonna head to Noah's trailer in a minute. He asked me to come out, and I don't like telling him no, unless I have a game. I don't want any confusion with her man, but I was hoping to at least speak to her. When she told me he wasn't cool with us talking every now and then, I knew I had to come just to bid our friendship farewell. I'm tryna be respectful and shit, but he don't even know that I could get to her without him getting within an inch of me if I wanted to."

My eyebrows lifted. I was hoping there wouldn't be any drama. The white people looked forward to that shit. Any moment where we embarrassed ourselves was highlighted in the news like it was priority. He continued. "Thankfully, I'm a changed man. I can respect how he feels, and I'll seek his permission before speaking to Jess. How much does he know about us?"

Jakari answered the question, but I just shrugged. My loyalty was to Brix, no matter how bad Jess did Nate. "He knows everything. Jess told him. She didn't need to keep any secrets from the man she plans to spend the rest of her life with. She would only be asking for trouble if he ever found out."

"Okay. That explains it then. I wouldn't be cool with my wife-to-be still maintaining a friendship with someone she slept with. I get it. I'm just gonna go chill in the trailer and do my best to avoid Jess altogether then. Damn."

He stood from his seat, and Jakari stood with him. "I'll be right back, D."

I gave him a head nod. Nate was under the impression that Brix didn't know and was just being a jealous ass nigga. Now it made sense. Jess didn't tell that man that she told Brix all the fucking details. She was gon' mess around and get somebody fucked up. I watched them make their way to Noah's trailer, but not before Jess came out of hers, wearing a short ass denim dress, boots, and a cowboy hat.

I immediately stood to look for Brix, because there was no way Nate could avoid her now. When I spotted him, he was staring right at them as they spoke. She extended her hand to Nate, and he gently shook it while I made my way to Brix. "You good?" I asked him.

"Yeah. He hasn't been disrespectful... yet."

"I don't think he will. She told him how you feel about them talking. He was actually heading to the trailer, trying to avoid seeing her up close."

Brix nodded as we watched Jess smile at Nate and say something to him then walk away. Nate didn't walk away as soon as she did. He watched her for a moment, then slowly shook his head before heading to the trailer with Noah. I could see Brix tensing up a bit, but he was cool. He walked away from me without a word, heading to where Jess was.

Jakari joined me as we headed back to my parents. "What did she say to him?"

Jakari smirked. "Just that she was happy to see him and hoped he enjoyed the production. It was innocent, but I could see the attraction in both their eyes, more so his than hers."

"Damn. I hate that she didn't tell him everything. Had he known all that, he probably wouldn't have come. You think she lowkey wanted to see him?"

"Possibly. She better be careful with that shit though. Nate has a career to worry about. She don't need to be putting him in positions like this," Jakari said as we sat.

We suspended the conversation for now as the rest of the family joined us. Grandma and Grandpa Henderson sat close to the dirt. She was getting extremely feeble, so I was surprised they even made it out. Tiffany was going to be putting on a show and had invited Malachi out to bull ride. Their rodeo friends, Legend, Red, and Zayson had also come out. Could have sworn this was a rodeo instead of a video shoot.

When the music started, Jess was in position, seated and watching the show Tiff's relay team was putting on as Noah and a friend made their way to the seats. I listened to the lyrics of the song to hear him say, *She a country hood shorty that lassoed my heart.* I smiled as I watched him sit close to her and stare at her like he wanted her. She noticed him and smiled.

The cameras panned out to catch some of the action as Jess stood to root Tiff and her team on. Noah made his way to her as he scanned her body. They exchanged words as he slid his arm around her waist before the director yelled, "Cut!"

Everyone clapped, and Jess quickly made her way to the trailer to change. They would be doing a stable scene next, riding horses on the other side without the crowd. Tiffany and her team, along with her daughter, Maui, Ashanni, Karima, and Malia would entertain the crowd until they were ready for Mal. As I scanned the crowd of family, Jakari asked, "Did you see her?"

"Who?"

"Tyeis is here. She's over there by Shylou and Cass."

"Naw. I hadn't seen her. I'm not really trying to see her. She gon' have me too soft."

He chuckled. I knew she would be here if her schedule permitted it. I sat back in the stadium-like seating as I watched Milana, Tiff's daughter, barrel race. It was like they were all competing against each other. Maui, Ashanni, and Malia weren't as advanced as Karima and Milana, but it was still entertaining. Karima was Kenny's daughter, and she'd been doing this longer than all of them. I believed she was like twenty-two now.

Maui was Storm's baby. She was fifteen and the sweetest of his kids. Ashanni was Jasper's oldest child. She was between Storm's twins and Maui in age. Lastly, Malia was Marcus's daughter. She was only twelve or so. She was the youngest but the hungriest. She got that hustle mentality from her father for sure.

As I watched them, I felt a presence standing near me. I looked up to see Tyeis. After taking a deep breath, I stood and greeted her. My mind was saying to ignore her, but my heart wouldn't allow that. It would have killed me to do that anyway. "Hey, Decaurey. How have you been?"

"Hey. Good. What about you?"

"I've been okay. Missing you."

I knew she would go there. She said she would be trying to get me back in her life, but she hadn't been overbearing. She hadn't texted since she put me on notice about the efforts she would be making to gain my heart. Although she was trying to give me space, she was still letting her intentions be made known. I missed her too, but I couldn't verbalize that right now. Instead, I asked, "Is Angel here with you?"

She lowered her head for a moment then looked back up at me. "No. She's spending today with some friends. She told me to tell you hello."

"Tell her I said what's up." Seeing her deflate in my presence was fucking with me, so I had to tell her, "I've missed you too."

Her eyes met mine as a slight smile formed on her lips. She nodded and was about to walk away until I grabbed her hand. She turned back to me, so I said, "Good to see you."

"You too."

I released her hand and watched her make her way back to Shylou before sitting. "Miserable ass," I heard someone say and chuckle.

I didn't have to look to see who said it. I already knew it was Storm. I rolled my eyes and took a deep breath as I looked over at Kenny. "Does your brother ever mind his business?"

Kenny laughed. "At this point, if he did, we would all be confused as to what could be wrong with him."

"Decaurey, you should be used to that shit by now," Jasper said and laughed.

"I have to keep shit interesting around here, but more importantly, as mayor, it's my job to be in everybody's shit. As your uncle, my presence makes your life better than what it was. Now when you gon' give yourself what you fiending for? Quit acting like a female. Get out your pitiful ass feelings and go get what you want."

I slowly shook my head at his bullshit, but he was right. I looked where Shylou was sitting but didn't see Tyeis anymore. If she left, I would leave well enough alone... for now.

## CHAPTER TWELVE

### TYEIS

My girl was fucking this shoot up. She and Noah looked like naturals. I'd journeyed to the other side to watch them create magic. They were riding horses, and Noah looked uncomfortable as hell at first. Jess had grabbed his hand, coaxing him to relax. Once he did, it was great. The cameras had never stopped, and I knew they would incorporate that into the video somehow. She was the country one, so it made sense.

Seeing Decaurey was so overwhelming. I couldn't stay in his presence any longer. When he grabbed my hand, I thought I was gonna pass out. I had to come over to this side to get a breather. His aura had swallowed me up and was threatening to drown me. Nothing else mattered at that moment. As much as I needed my phone, that shit could die, and I wouldn't even notice. He had my undivided attention.

His gaze had held me captive. After he said he missed me too, I could have melted to the ground. However, I wasn't naïve. I knew that didn't mean he wanted me back in his life as his woman. Knowing that he missed me still felt good though. I didn't want to overstay my welcome in his presence, so I had to get away from him, although it seemed like he wasn't ready for me to.

I was trying not to rush him. I'd been taking my medicine religiously for the past two weeks. Thankfully, I hadn't had another bout of insomnia. It was killing me not to reach out more. I sent gifts so he would know I was thinking about him but trying to respect his wishes at the same time. I knew he would love the gifts I bought, and I noticed he was wearing the belt buckle today.

As I watched Noah pull my girl in his arms and grab a handful of the cake she had stuffed in the jeans she'd changed into, my phone started to vibrate. I stepped away to answer it. When I pulled it from my pocket, I saw it was Tyrese. He'd been blowing me up for the past two weeks, probably wondering what the fuck happened to me. He usually heard from me at least once a week when I wasn't busy. Even then, I would text him and let him know that I was out of pocket.

I ignored the call and brought my attention back to Jess. I was so damn proud of her. Had it not been for my inconsistency with taking my meds, I knew I could probably get more jobs like this. While I knew her getting this job had nothing to do with Shylou, I knew I could network more with Houston's rappers and make my way onto the scene. Me not taking my meds like I should made me a liability. At least, that was the way I saw it. I believed that was how Shy saw it as well, whether he said so or not.

When Noah leaned over and kissed Jess's lips, I could tell she wasn't as comfortable. She was such a sexual person. Knowing her, she'd gotten turned on. Brix was standing there watching with a slight frown on his face. Jess had said it didn't take much to send him into possessive mode, so I knew he was having a fucking fit that Nate was here. If he only knew how much Jess cut for him, he would be the chillest nigga here. She was still talking to Nate occasionally, but she told me they had established an amazing friendship.

However, I thought it best for her to end that as well, since she'd told Brix about their past. If she wanted to keep him as a friend, she should have kept that shit to herself. She'd told me how amazing sex was with him. Had it not been for her history with Brix, she would have undoubtedly been Nate's woman, living in Dallas with him.

When the director yelled for them to cut, Jess smiled at Noah, and they went their separate ways. She ran right to Brix's arms. Jess was my best friend, but I sometimes found myself envying her. Here I was, trying to keep a man, and her options were endless. I loved that for her, but I wished I could at least have a man that wanted me without me self-sabotaging shit.

I watched him grab her cake the same way Noah did, as if showing everyone watching who it really belonged to and kiss her lips. She quickly got away from him before she couldn't as I chuckled. They still had one more rodeo scene to shoot. After that one, they would be going to the family barn right up the street to shoot a romantic scene. I turned to head back to the arena and nearly ran right into Storm. "I'm so sorry, Uncle Mayor."

He grinned hard and nodded. As I walked past him, he yelled back, "Go get yo' man. Be aggressive with his ass."

I frowned slightly. From the stories I heard about him, I knew not to take him seriously. I didn't know him well enough to know when he was serious and when he wasn't. Instead of voicing all that and having him curse me out, I nodded. When I got back to where Shylou and Cass were seated, I sat and said, "She is working the fuck out of this shoot. You and Carter should be so proud."

"I am. It's hard to believe though. I've known her since she was a little girl. I never imagined she would grow up to be a beautiful thirty something year old woman, modeling some of my shit."

Cass shoulder bumped him with a frown on her face. "I mean our shit. My bad, Cass Styles."

His clothing line was named after his wife; plus, she designed some of the pieces Jess and I wore. He leaned over and kissed her on the lips. Every woman here was coupled up, and it was making me depressed. Even a couple of Jess's younger cousins had boyfriends here. They were all hugged up, especially Karima. He congratulated her on doing her thing earlier, and I found myself entranced by their display of affection.

As I watched Malachi prepare to put on a show, I watched the other men surrounding him, helping him. One particular one was talking more to him and laughing. He was dark skinned and sexy as fuck. When he demonstrated to Malachi the stance he should be in on the bull, I knew he was the bull extraordinaire Shylou had mentioned earlier, Legend Semien. *Good Lord.* The Lord blessed every man here with swag. All of them made having a preference sound stupid.

As I continued watching them and then seeing Noah talking to them, I knew that at some point, Jessica was gonna grab those dreads. I giggled at the thought of it. She used to always say that if she ever dated a man with dreads, he would get tired of her putting her hands in them. I thought she was gonna grab them when he kissed her.

Just as I was about to reach into my pocket for my phone to check on Angel, I saw Decaurey coming toward me. My heart rate skyrocketed. I was trying to play it cool, though, because he could be going talk to someone else or coming over here to speak to Shylou. I didn't tear my gaze away from him though. I was never shy about admiring a gorgeous man.

When he got close, he spoke to Shylou and Cass, then brought his attention to me. "Can we talk?"

"Yeah. Sure."

He grabbed my hand, and I stood from my seat then pulled up my tube top. I watched his eyes travel to my breasts before he led the way out, still holding my hand. When we got somewhere a little more private, he said, "Someone told me that if I think about you every day, I should give us another chance. I'll just be miserable if I don't. While I don't feel like I should just dive right back in, I do want to talk to you more often, if that's cool."

"Why wouldn't I be cool with that, Decaurey? You know I want you back, and that's a step in that direction. I've really missed you," I said as I brought my hand to his cheek.

He grabbed my hand and kissed it, causing things below to stir. "Come sit with me. How have things really been going?" he asked as he pulled me toward where he was sitting.

"Things have been good. I've been consistently taking my medication. Thankfully, I haven't had another issue with insomnia. That seems to be the only time I want to stop taking my meds. I had to convince myself that I could make it on my own and there would be brighter days. I would be blessed for every tear I cried and every time I tried to do what was best for me," I said, somewhat quoting Lalah Hathaway.

"On Your Own" had become my song of inspiration. When I faced moments where I felt like giving up these past two weeks, I would listen to that. I was basing the stability of my mental health on people instead of me. I was the one in control, especially when I took my medication. I knew there would be times that it would feel like I wasn't in control, but that was where my resilience would have to shine through.

Although I didn't get diagnosed until I was in my junior year in high school, I knew as a preteen that something wasn't right. I didn't know how to articulate what was going on with me though. The symptoms were mild back then, but as I got older, they showed more of themselves. Once I got checked at seventeen, they told me that I was a manic depressive.

"I'm proud of you, Tyeis. I do want what's best for you. If you feel yourself struggling with it, you can call me. I don't mind."

I nodded as we sat. Storm looked back at us and winked, causing Decaurey to smile. I wasn't much of a smiler unless I was extremely happy, but I offered him a slight smile as well. Decaurey grabbed my hand and said, "What I said someone said to me about if I think about you every day actually came from Storm. Can you believe that?"

"Hell no. He told me today to go get my man, but I didn't know if

I should take him seriously. I didn't want him setting me up for failure."

Decaurey chuckled. "I definitely understand. You don't know him like I do, and I still hesitate at his advice."

I chuckled. Great advice came from an unsuspecting source this time. "What's up, Ty?"

I turned to see Nesha approaching me. Standing from my seat, I reached out and touched her belly. It seemed it had grown overnight. It had only been two weeks since I'd last seen her. As I rubbed her belly, she giggled. "Do y'all know what you're having yet?" I asked.

"Not yet," she said as Lennox kissed her head. "We find out at my next appointment."

"Okay. Were you not feeling well? Is that why y'all are just getting here?"

"The heat was getting to me. We were sitting in Jessica's trailer. She looked so beautiful."

"I know. I'm so proud of her."

Nesha and Lennox sat on the other side of Jakari after he stood and hugged me, then we turned our attention to the dirt. Malachi was about to ride. Noah and Jessica were walking in, and he was doing his best to focus on Jess. I could tell that he was new to country shit like this. Once they were seated next to Jessica's grandparents, one of the guys over there with Malachi swung the gate open.

That bull was bucking like it was out for blood. Jess stood and cheered for Mal like we were at a real rodeo, along with everyone else. What I learned about the Hendersons was that they supported their own and anyone close enough to be considered family. Once the buzzer sounded and Malachi was still going, everyone was on their feet. Mal hopped off the first opportunity he got as the rodeo clowns closed in to distract the bull.

When Noah turned to Jess, I could see how wide his eyes were. She was laughing at his excitement. I glanced over to the side area to see Nate standing there watching, then he walked off. This trip had to be miserable for him. He came to watch a shoot but couldn't for fear he would stare at Jess too long and offend Brix. *Damn.*

Once they ended this scene, Jess and Noah were whisked away to change for the last time for their romantic scene. I would love to be a fly on the wall for that one. They were only allowing Noah's people to go and Shylou. They didn't want anyone distracting Jess. At the "rodeo" and horse riding, she was in her element. There wasn't much she could do to mess it up. This dinner would be totally different.

If Noah was who I thought he was and who he portrayed himself to be in the many interviews he'd done, I knew he would help her through it. He seemed to be a really nice guy… Godly, although some of his songs were anything but. He was sexy as hell too. A man that loved the Lord that much but still had a little bit of Satan in him was attractive. He was like David in the Bible. The man was the apple of God's eye, but slept with another man's wife, then had the man put on the front lines to get killed.

Shit, Noah had a song called "Apple of God's Eye" some years back if I wasn't mistaken. People like Noah proved God was real, but that it was still okay to be human. I loved that about him. People equated Christianity with perfection, and Lord have mercy did they have it all wrong. Some Christians equated it that way too. That was why they felt they had a right to judge others. However, Noah made being filled with the love of God cool.

When Decaurey grabbed my hand, I turned to him. "You good? You got quiet on me."

"I'm okay," I said as I gave his hand a reassuring squeeze.

I was better than good. While I was hoping to have time with him, I didn't imagine it would be this way. Being in his presence made everything okay. My nervous jitters were nonexistent now, and I was more relaxed than I had been since we met. "How long will you be in town?"

"I'm leaving tonight. I'm not prepared to stay. Had I known this would go this way, I would have insisted that Angel come with me, and we stay the night."

"Well, are you gonna at least stay to eat?"

"Umm... who can pass up Mrs. Jen's food like that? I surely can't. Ain't no way."

He chuckled as he intertwined his fingers with mine. "I'm glad you're here, Ty. For real."

When he leaned over and kissed my lips, I closed my eyes and prayed that I didn't fuck up again. This couldn't be the last time I felt his lips. I needed him, and I wouldn't rest until he was mine again.

## CHAPTER THIRTEEN

### DECAUREY

"Oh fuck! I missed this pussy, Ty! Shit!"

Just as I figured, I was soft as cotton around her ass. All she had to do was rub my chest just right, and now she was in my bed with her ass tooted up and twerking on my dick. "Decaurey! Oh my God!"

I shoved her face in the bed because she was loud as fuck. I didn't know how we got from sitting down to eat some beef tips to here, but shit, I wasn't mad about it. The problem would be if she went back to acting how she'd been acting lately. I couldn't even lie and say this was her fault. This shit was all me. Sitting around Lennox and Nesha, Jess and Brix, and all my uncles and aunts had me in my feelings big time.

The only people, besides the kids and our younger adult cousins, who weren't paired up were Jakari, Noah, and Nate. Noah had a wife. She just wasn't there. Nate was doing his best to not look at Jess, but I caught him staring a couple of times. Jakari was busy being a fool, so he didn't have time to be in his feelings like me. Just watching Ty lick her fingers had me bricked up something serious. I asked her to take a ride with me, and we ended up butt ass naked.

"Ty, I'm 'bout to bust, baby."

She pulled away from me and quickly turned around and put her mouth on my dick, sucking the fucking excitement right out of me. She had me in here practically screaming like a bitch because she wouldn't let go until he was hard again. She fell back onto the bed when the vice grips she called jaws released me. She grabbed her ankles and spread her legs open for me. *Damn*. I wanted her so bad. I needed her to stay cool though so we could get along more than just to fuck each other senseless.

Grabbing the lube from my nightstand, I waved it in the air and asked, "You down?"

"I'm down for anything you wanna do."

"I won't be angry if you say no. You don't have to agree to everything I want to do simply because you feel like you need to make things up to me."

"Decaurey, shut up, and come fuck me in the ass. You gotta lick it first though."

"You ain't said nothing but a word. I'm 'bout to eat them groceries like it's a T-bone."

I made my way to her ass and lightly licked over the hole and watched her tremble. I did it again and her pussy literally quivered. She had me about to bust without being inside of her. I slid my tongue in her asshole and watched her squirm then pushed my fingers in her pussy. Within seconds, she was spraying that good shit all over the place and doing her best to remain quiet. "Scream if you need to, baby. Let those muthafuckas know you being thoroughly pleased. Fuck them."

I went back to lick her ass, but she scooted away from me slightly. "Take me now, before I lose the nerve. My pussy can barely handle your dick. You better make me cum so good until I black out too."

"Mm. I work best under pressure," I said as I rubbed lube over her asshole and massaged my dick with it.

He was already leaking and twitching with excitement just from anticipating how good this was about to be. I went straight up on my knees and rubbed my dick over her asshole as she closed her eyes. "Relax and breathe. I'll give you a little at a time so you will know what you can handle."

I pushed inside of her, and she tensed up immediately, then relaxed her muscles just as quickly. Once I completely got the head of my dick inside of her, I was sweating like I'd run a five-mile marathon. Pushing another inch or so inside of her, I watched her face scrunch up for a moment. I pulled out some and began stroking her, working more of my dick inside of her as she moaned loudly. "Decaurey, I've never felt something that hurts so fucking good."

I bit my bottom lip as I leaned over her and pushed even more inside of her. She gripped my arm as I stilled my movements. I'd gotten half my dick inside of her. I was content with that shit. She didn't have to take another centimeter. As I stroked her ass, my eyes rolled to the back of my head. My dick was enjoying every moment of this, and by the way Ty was moaning and pinching her nipples, she was enjoying it too.

I licked my thumb and began playing with her clit, trying to make sure she had the ultimate stimulation. "Decaurey! Oh shit!"

Her asshole got wet as hell and her body froze. When her eyes rolled, I knew this was it. Her anal orgasm had arrived. I started stroking her feverishly while her body flopped around like a fish out of water. This shit was amazing to watch. Knowing that I could please her the way I did was an ego booster like none other. When her body started to calm down, I released my nut in her ass and nearly collapsed on top of her.

I turned my head toward her, and just like she'd requested, her ass had blacked out.

WHEN I OPENED MY EYES, Tyeis was no longer in bed. I sat up, thinking she'd left, but I heard the shower running. It was only ten o'clock, but I knew she needed to get back to Houston tonight. I got out of bed and made my way to the bathroom to shower with her. When I walked in, she was standing in front of the mirror, staring at her body, analyzing the hanging flesh at her midsection. She was probably still trying to decide if she would undergo another surgery. With the industry she was in, I could see why it mattered to her.

I leaned against the doorframe, admiring her beauty. All that superficial shit didn't matter to me. Her heart, her mind, and her pussy were my main concerns. Sometimes one took precedence over the other, depending on the situation the moment called for. She looked over at me and gave me a big smile. That was so unlike her. She rarely showed her teeth when she smiled. I didn't know why, because it was beautiful. "Looks like you knocked yourself out too," she said and chuckled.

"Hell yeah. That shit was so good."

"It was. I really wish I could stay. Angel has called three times. That was what woke me up. I told her I would be leaving in the next hour."

"Mm. Well I better get in here and clean up good so I can feel that pussy once more before you go."

She bit her bottom lip as she stared at me. I licked my lips and grabbed her hand, leading her to the shower. The moment we were inside, she wrapped her arms around me and laid her head on my shoulder. I kissed her forehead, then said, "I apologize for taking us here tonight. It went against everything I said earlier and what you agreed to."

She lifted her head and gave me a soft smile. Stroking my cheek with the back of her hand, she said, "I know how to say no, Decaurey. I want to be with you... whatever that looks like. I trust you completely, and if you are willing to move us along faster than you originally planned, I have no objections."

I chuckled then kissed her lips. "Let's get cleaned up, baby."

As I washed her body with the Dove soap she'd left here two weeks ago, I said, "I'm glad you're putting your mental health to the forefront. For the record, my decisions had nothing to do with that. I know what mental illness looks like, especially depression. You know about my issues with it, but I watched my mother struggle a bit with it after her divorce years ago. She made that shit look easy to deal with, but I know that's what mothers tend to do for their kids."

I stooped and kissed her leg then began washing it. "She tried to pretend that she was okay in front of me, but she didn't know that I'd seen her tears when she thought I wasn't watching. On the weekends, she would stay in bed practically the entire time. I was a teenager and always had shit to do, but I paid attention to her. I plan to help you with whatever struggles you face. I just need you to be open with me about how you're feeling. If you can do that, I'll always be here."

I stared up at her after washing her foot and journeying to her other leg. Her lips were turned up like she would cry at any moment. She lowered her gaze to mine and nodded as a tear fell down her cheek. "I promise. I've never had anyone to make me feel the way you do, not even bitch ass Kelvin."

I frowned slightly as she said, "Angel's father."

"Oh. I don't remember you ever telling me his name."

"Yeah. So whatever I have to do to assure that you won't leave me again, I'll do that. I trust you, so I know you won't have me doing anything ridiculous. I know you care about me a lot. I want you to one day love me."

I stood and kissed her lips. "If our lines of communication stay open and we work out our issues logically, when possible, I will fall in love with you. Your heart is good, Tyeis. That's what matters most to me. I like your feistiness. It keeps things interesting. I love how you can be outspoken and outgoing at times. You know I like a straight shooter and a good turn up. Just please don't lie to me. We will be able to work through almost anything if you just keep it real with me."

I was already in love with her. I knew it the moment I slid into her paradise tonight. It was why I couldn't resist her. It was way more than just being sprung. Her pussy was good as hell, but I'd had good pussy before. It came a dime a dozen. She was offering the other shit I needed too... like Tammy. Although that shit took years to find again, I'd found it. It didn't help that I fell easily. I was naturally a romantic, and I wanted Ty to eventually meet that side of me.

"Thank you for giving me a chance to get it right. Falling in love with you will be easy. I haven't been in love in a long time, but I know that I want to fall in love with you. I feel like I'm already on my way there."

I kissed her lips again then she grabbed my body wash and began lathering my towel. As I was about to take it from her, she said, "No. Let me do this for you, baby."

I bit my bottom lip and nodded, watching her take care of me in ways I never had. I'd never been washed by a woman before, and I realized I'd been missing out. Feeling her hands grace every part of me was an aphrodisiac like no other. When she began washing my dick, he grew to full potential. He was already hard, but now my erection was getting painful. It was like I didn't have enough skin for him to grow into.

She stroked him with the soapy towel then moved behind me to where I could rinse off. Her arms slid around my waist as her titties pressed against my back. "I think I'm going to have surgery. A fupa tuck and a titty lift."

I wanted to laugh at her choice of words, but somehow, I was able to hold it in. "Whatever makes you happy. Just let me know when so I can be there to take care of you. Storm would be happy to oversee my workers. He does that shit anyway."

She giggled. "What did I do to deserve you?"

"Be yourself. You deserve so much more than what I can even

offer though. I'm just grateful you and Jess even became friends so we could meet."

She smiled and nodded as I rinsed off once more, being sure to rinse my dick off thoroughly. "Do we have time, Ty? I don't wanna hold you up. If you need me to wait, I can."

"I always have time for you."

After her words of confirmation, I lifted her against the shower wall and lowered her on my dick. Her head dropped back as she arched her back, and I lowered my head to lick and suck her nipples. I wasn't trying to knock the bottom out this time. I wanted to make love to her. I wanted her to *feel* all the things I refused to say right now. It was time to get back to love... the journey we were on before all the drama and miscommunication.

Those three months of talking to her without seeing her had exposed my heart and not just my dick to her personality and aura. I didn't even realize it at the time, but I surely knew now. I stroked her slowly but deeply and intentionally. Every stroke had purpose, and I wanted her to know how much she meant to me with every inch that penetrated her.

"Decaurey," she whispered. "I'm... cumming!"

Her nails dug into my back, and I brought my lips to her neck, kissing then gently biting it as her juices flooded me like a baptism. The feeling was definitely spiritual. At that moment, I could foresee the future. If we continued the path we were on, life was about to become the best it had ever been. My finances were straight, my business was consistently growing, and now, love had found me once again.

The closer I got to nutting, the harder it became to keep my same pace. I was struggling. As if I weren't struggling enough, Tyeis damn near closed her walls around me like she'd done once before, but this time, I didn't have time to pull out. I fired off within her depths. Her eyes opened slowly, and she stared at me as I stared right back. No words were spoken for a minute, then she put me out of my misery by saying, "I'm on the pill, Decaurey."

I started tickling her as she slid from my arms, screaming in laughter. "You were tryna see me sweat, weren't you? Don't play with me, girl. I only sweat when I'm pouring cement."

She laughed more. "You sweat when you're working out too, no matter what that workout entails."

She bit her bottom lip then grabbed her towel from the holder and washed between her legs. "Uh huh. You play too much," I responded then smacked her wet ass.

Her eyes widened when she turned to me. "That shit hurt! That's yo' ass!"

I was stuck. I hadn't washed my dick off yet, but I was about to hop out of that shower so quick. I opened the door, and she caught me right on the ass with that towel. That shit stung the voice right out of me... had my fucking voice box on pause. She laughed so loud. That shit was gonna leave a welt. When my voice finally came through, I yelled in a high-pitched voice, "Shit!"

I swore I sounded like Jim Carey in the movie *Liar Liar* when he got pulled over by the police. That shit only made Tyeis laugh more. I had to carry my ass back in there, though, so I could wash up. When I got in front of the mirror, I glanced back like a fucking female to see my ass cheeks were red. That towel had caught both of 'em.

When I got in the shower, she wiped the smile off her face, and said, "I'm so sorry, baby."

"Get away from me, gangsta."

That only caused her to laugh more. She wrapped her arms around me and kissed my uncooperative lips. When her hand touched my ass, I flinched. "You have some Neosporin I can put on it?"

I frowned at her. "First of all, no. Secondly, ain't nothing that feel like oil or lube going anywhere near my ass. Now back up."

She laughed as she nearly fell in the tub. "See, karma was about to take yo' ass out."

I kissed her lips, grateful that we could not only fuck each other, but we could laugh together. This had to be everything I thought it was, because if it weren't, I would probably be done with relationships forever.

## CHAPTER FOURTEEN

### TYEIS

"I'm in a relationship now. I'm sorry I didn't call and say something sooner. I just wasn't sure of where we were going, and I didn't want to complicate things by being with you."

"Damn, girl. So you telling me I gotta find another fuck buddy? We been fucking around for the past, what, three years?"

"I don't know, but I'm happy with where I am now, Tyrese. I don't want anything to come between that. So I knew it was best that I contacted you and put you up on notice."

"Put me on notice, huh? What if I don't want us to be done, Ty?"

I pulled the phone from my ear and stared at it with a frown on my face like he could see me. *This nigga need to get it together.* "Umm... you don't have a choice. I would have to be a willing participant. We had a good run, but I have to move on."

"So I can't even get one for the road and go out with a bang?"

I rolled my eyes. It would only be a reminder that Decaurey had a bigger dick and better skills. "Naw, that's not gon' work. But you take care, okay?"

I ended the call and huffed loudly. After I got home Saturday night, I crashed. I was sore as hell the next day, so I spent the day at the spa. I took Angel with me, and we enjoyed our girl time. Now, a week later, I was in New Orleans, enjoying a shoot on Bourbon Street. My baby had come with me to the shoot. I felt like she wanted to come to make sure I stayed in pocket. It had been a week since I saw Decaurey, and I was a little in my feelings.

He told me once he got his guys situated on a big job, he would be able to spend quite a bit of time with me. This living in different cities was for the fucking birds. I just wanted to enjoy time laying in his arms at least. FaceTiming was cool, but that shit got old. He could've come to see me Friday, but our flights out for Nawlins left Thursday evening. Here it was, Saturday evening, and besides the amazing time at the photo shoot, I was feeling miserable.

When we left the magazine shoot, we went to a place called Olde Nola Cookery, complements of the magazine. They were highlighting full-figured models in the south, particularly in Texas. Jess had done a shoot with them while she was in Brazil. I was grateful that they recognized my place in this industry. It had been a grueling, steady climb, but the point was that it was a climb and not a fall.

Once we were done eating, we went back to our hotel room. The first thing I did was shower and got all this makeup off my face. I was ready to just relax, and I believed Angel was on the same type of time that I was on. As soon as I got out of the shower, she was hopping in. It was hot and sticky. It was usually that way in Houston too, but because the shoot was outside, we were really drained.

As she showered, there was a knock on the door. I frowned, because I typically didn't have visitors at my hotel rooms when I was out of town unless it was planned. I sat still for a moment, waiting to see if maybe they had the wrong room. When they knocked again, I got up and peeked out of the peephole. I didn't see anyone. I refused to open the door to look. People were crazy as fuck these days.

I made stomping noises then stepped away from the door but stayed close just in case they knocked again. I leaned against the wall for a moment, then quietly went back to the door and saw Tyrese standing there about to knock again. What in the fuck was he doing here? Furthermore, how in the fuck did he know where I was? I refused to open that door, especially with my daughter here. He was stalking me, and that shit was dangerous.

I went back to the bed and called Decaurey, but he didn't answer. Thankfully, I had Nesha's number. Maybe her husband Lennox could give me advice on what to do since he was a detective. "Hello?"

"Hey, Nesha. This is Tyeis."

"Hey, girl! What's up?"

"I have a slight situation that I need Lennox's advice on."

"Don't tell me you took Decaurey outta here," she said and laughed. "I'm just kidding. You sound serious. Let me get the phone to him."

Within a few seconds, Lennox answered. "Hey, Ty. What's up?"

"Hey. I think I have a stalker. Should I call the police in New Orleans? We're both from Houston. He's knocking on my door, but I didn't tell him where I was going."

"If that's the case, you can call the police there to get him away from you, but when you get back home, file a restraining order on him there too."

"Thanks, Lennox. I'm going to do that now."

"I have a friend that works for the New Orleans Police Department. Actually, he's the chief. Let me give him a call and send him to you. Send Nesha your location."

"Oh my goodness. Thank you so much."

"No problem."

I ended the call and quickly texted Nesha my location. As soon as I was done, someone was knocking at the door again. I was ready to go the fuck off on his ass, but I didn't want to alert Tyrese that I knew it was him. Quietly, I made my way to the door to check the peephole. When I saw Decaurey standing there, I nearly lost my shit. I quickly opened the door and threw myself into him as he laughed.

"Damn. I guess you happy to see me, huh?"

"Yes! I missed you like crazy!" I said as the tears fell from my eyes.

He frowned slightly as he wiped them away. "You okay?"

I shook my head rapidly. "I'm being stalked. He probably saw you."

"You know who *he* is?" he asked as he turned back toward the door.

"Yeah. I told him I had a boyfriend, and I could no longer be in contact with him. He was blowing my damn phone up. We were fuck buddies. I really didn't owe him an explanation since we never really engaged in casual conversation, but I didn't want him to say he didn't know. He basically said he wasn't ready to end what we had. I hung up on him at that point. I didn't think it would lead to this though," I rattled off.

"When was the last time y'all were together? When did you last see him today?" he asked.

"Over a month ago now... maybe over two. He was at the door, playing games about five or ten minutes before you got here. He'd knock, and when I went to the door, he would disappear. It was like he wanted me to open the door so he could force his way in here. I called Nesha, and Lennox said he knows the police chief out here. He's sending him here."

"How do you know it was him, baby?"

I frowned slightly. Was he doubting that I saw him? "I stomped away from the door but went back quietly and saw his ass standing there. Why are you asking all these questions? You don't believe me?"

"I believe you, baby. I just wanted details," he said, pulling me into his arms and kissing my head.

"I'm glad you're here. I suppose Angel told you where we were."

"Yeah, she did. He doesn't have access to her, does he?"

I pulled away from him. "No. You're the only man I've ever dealt with that has her number, besides bitch ass Kelvin."

His eyebrows lifted. I knew why. I'd told him that she had never interacted with him. "Yeah. She ended up befriending her damn brother in D.C., and he gave her number to their dad."

"Damn. That's a crazy way to meet a sibling."

"Right. She found out that he was the jackass I'd warned her about. But she also learned that he left because of her diagnosis instead of mine. I hate that."

"Does she seem to be handling it okay, though?"

"Yeah. Better than me."

"Everything is going to be okay. I'm here and after dinner, I'll hold you all night. Are you cool with me sleeping in here with y'all? I know Angel being here makes things different. I can get another room."

"I think it will be okay. She's really comfortable with you, and so am I."

"Okay. Well let me go check the hallways and shit for this nigga and get my bag."

"Be careful, Decaurey. Jess said you can't fight."

He frowned as I relaxed some and laughed. "Bestie Jessie gon' get told off when I get back."

"She was just playing. I believe you can handle your own when need be."

"Fa sho. You have a picture of what this nigga looks like?"

"I have him on Facebook."

I went to his profile and showed Decaurey. He frowned as he stared at him. "I've seen this nigga before. I'm just not sure where."

My eyebrows lifted. I didn't know where he would have seen him either. He stood there thinking for a moment then looked at his picture again. "Hmm. Okay. I'll be right back, baby."

"Okay."

I watched him leave the room, making sure the door closed behind him. I was more at ease with him here. Him surprising me out here was just what I needed. Although we couldn't engage in extracurricular activities, I was just happy for his presence. The bathroom door opened, and Angel came out looking refreshed. "I feel sooo much better," she said.

I smiled at her. "Thank you for making sure Decaurey made it to us."

She smiled. "Where is he?"

"He went to get his bag. I told him he could stay in here with us. Is that okay with you?"

"Yeah! We can watch *Hunter X Hunter*! I can cast it to the TV."

I rolled my eyes as she giggled. The knock at the door made me tense up. I quickly got up before Angel could run to the door to see Decaurey standing there, checking his surroundings. I opened it, and he quickly walked in and made sure it closed. When he came around the corner, Angel ran to him. She hugged him tightly, and that made me smile.

"Hey, D! Glad you made it!"

"What's up, Cherubim?"

I frowned as she giggled. "Cherubim?"

"Yeah. That's an angel that's close to God and protects His way. This lil angel is perfect for that."

He kissed her head as she pulled him further into the room. I smiled at how excited she was to have him here. She released his hand and hopped in her bed as he stood in front of me. "You look like you can get a nap in. How was the shoot?"

"I need a nap in the worst way. The shoot was good but tiring. I'll be doing the interview tomorrow before our flight leaves."

"Okay. Well, come on."

He pulled his polo-styled shirt over his head, revealing a white tee, and got in bed with me. He wrapped his arms around me and held me tightly in his embrace as I drifted off into dreamland.

AFTER WE WERE SEATED at Deanie's Seafood, I took in the ambiance of the restaurant. It was dimly lit, but it seemed casual enough. I wore a dress and so did Angel. Decaurey had worn slacks and a nice shirt. It wasn't a place I would feel comfortable wearing denim shorts to. I was just ready for some authentic Cajun food. While Southeast Texas had authentic Cajun food, it was just different eating it in New Orleans.

Most of Southeast Texas residents had roots in Louisiana, at least the black ones. Decaurey had told me that his mom was from a small town in Southwest Louisiana called Cankton. It wasn't far from Lafayette. So I was pretty sure he'd eaten this type of food all his life. He'd explained to me that some foods tasted different though. He said New Orleans gumbo didn't taste like the gumbo he grew up on in Southwest Louisiana.

He was convinced that New Orleans citizens were Creole and Southwest Louisiana were Cajuns. Hell, I thought they were the same thing, so I had to look the shit up for myself. Although I knew the internet didn't always have shit right, I figured I could filter through what was correct and what wasn't. It said that Creoles were mostly black and mixed-race people while Cajuns were white. Decaurey was far from white, personality-wise.

With further research, it said Creoles populated New Orleans, and Cajuns populated the more rural areas. There were definitely black people in rural Louisiana. I was sure a lot of them had white folks somewhere in their heritage, as did everyone else. If that were the case, black people could definitely be Cajun. With as high yellow as Decaurey was, I was more than sure someone in his family tree was white, and it probably wasn't as far down the line as I originally thought.

Before we left the hotel room, Lennox's friend, Joe Stevenson, had come to our room to take a report. I told him everything I knew about Tyrese and how he had been blowing up my phone before I spoke to him about ending what we had. I also told him how Tyrese responded, which possibly was him warning me that he would be stalking my ass. He promised me that they would be looking for him, if for nothing else but to watch him.

When those people set that crawfish étouffée and fried shrimp in front of me, I nearly had a food-gasm. It smelled divine, and it looked amazing. I heard a chuckle, so I looked over at Decaurey to find him staring at me. "What?" I asked with a frown.

"Girl, you staring at that food like you finna fuck that shit up."

I chuckled. "I am. Are we looking at the same food?"

He laughed, too, as he brought his attention back to his gumbo, fried catfish, and oysters. Angel was quietly watching us with a smile on her face. She hadn't seen me this happy in a while, and I knew that made her love Decaurey even more.

As we ate, I felt a presence standing over me. I turned toward the person, assuming it was our waiter, coming to see if we needed anything more. I was shocked when I saw Tyrese standing there. My blood started to boil as I stared at him. "Excuse me. Can I speak to you, Tyeis?"

Decaurey stood from his seat and stared at Tyrese like he had shit on him and was threatening to drop it in our food. I frowned, and said, "Hell no! I'm on a date with my boyfriend and daughter! I told you I was done with you. Why are you following me? I filed a restraining order against you!"

The restaurant manager had come to our table, and Decaurey explained what the issue was. I could feel myself slipping though. I wanted to grab Tyrese by his fucking neck and sling him across the table. He wasn't as thick as Decaurey. He was on the slender side but was packing what I thought was a big dick until I met the unlawful anaconda Decaurey was packing around.

"Tyeis, why you wanna do this to us? This nigga can't treat you better than me. He can't dick you down like you like it. He's a kid compared to me. You can't tell me he's as experienced with pleasing your body as I am."

I frowned. How in the fuck did he know Decaurey's age? Decaurey's frown was as deep as mine as he said, "Who the fuck are you, and how do I know you?"

Tyrese smirked as we heard sirens in the distance. All eyes were on us. The security guard was more afraid than Angel and me. He was just standing off to the side, watching it unfold like everyone else. "Remember the good ol' reverend? That's my father."

Decaurey frowned even harder. "My mom's ex-husband didn't have any kids. What the fuck you on?"

"That was what he led y'all to believe. When I found out you were who Tyeis was falling for, I knew I had to stop this shit. Ain't no way she needs to fall victim to an entitled, privileged nigga that ain't got shit without his mama. She still got her tit in your mouth?"

I couldn't take it any longer. The police were taking too fucking long to come defuse this situation. I lunged at Tyrese, scratching the fuck out of him. My nails broke the skin with every swing of my hand. They were pointed and looked like claws. I could hear Angel screaming, but I couldn't make myself stop. Decaurey pulled me away from him and stood in front of me. Tyrese swung on Decaurey, and that created a whole ass mess.

They fell on the table, fighting as I pulled Angel out of the way. People were screaming and leaving the restaurant, totally appalled at what was happening. I was beyond pissed. It was like steam was rising from my collar. Decaurey was getting the best of him when the police rushed in like they were about to break up a gang fight. It was two niggas, and they came in with shields and their weapons drawn.

I started screaming for them to stop. Tyrese was a whole bitch for the drama he created over his jealousy, but I still didn't want to see him dead at the hands of the police. The cops were yelling at them to stop. Finally, Decaurey kicked him, making him double over, then stood and lifted his hands. I just couldn't believe all this shit had gone down.

"How a nigga gon' take care of a child that ain't his, but wasn't taking care of his own flesh and blood? I've hated you for a long time."

"I didn't have shit to do with his actions. He was a grown ass man. Your qualms should be with him, not me!"

Decaurey was shifting his jaw like it had popped out of place as a police officer stood next to him. "Your cousin, Lennox Guilman, is the reason you aren't in cuffs right now. He called and briefed us on the situation. I'm calling an ambulance to get you to a hospital. Your jaw is definitely out of place and needs to be popped back in."

All this shit was my fault, and I could tell that Decaurey thought so too by the way he was staring at me. "I don't know him from my mom's ex-husband. I've seen his ass somewhere else," he said through clenched teeth.

Angel wrapped her arms around me, and that somewhat brought me back from the edge. I wanted to go kick that muthafucka in his mouth. He ruined our evening, an evening that was supposed to bring us closer together as a family. *Why couldn't shit just go right?* It was like trouble looked for me so it could wreak havoc in my life. I learned that my medication was less effective in high intensity situations. This was definitely one of those situations.

As the police cuffed Tyrese, I went to him and punched him in his jaw. "If my man jaw is broken, yours needs to be the same way or worse, bitch."

The police grabbed me and cuffed me after that, while Decaurey silently fumed. I could see the anger in his eyes. His entire face was red, and he was frowning hard. When I stared into his eyes, he slowly shook his head and gave me a slight smirk, putting my nerves at ease. I thought he was angry at me. If he was, I didn't know how I would handle that.

## CHAPTER FIFTEEN

### DECAUREY

I knew that muthafucka from somewhere, and that shit was eating me alive. Despite the fact he was my ex-stepfather's illegitimate son, I knew it was something else going on as to why he was fucking with Ty. He was definitely trying to get to me. Although he was her fuck buddy at one time, I couldn't be angry about that. She was sleeping with him before she committed to being in a relationship with me.

I was at the police station since Tyeis decided to take matters into her own hands. Once we left from here, I would go to the hospital. Angel was seated close to me, and I could feel her trembling. I put my arm around her and asked through clenched teeth, "You okay?"

She quickly shook her head. "I'm scared. What are they doing to my mama?"

"They are probably asking her questions about what happened and why she felt the need to assault that guy once he was already subdued."

My mouth was killing me, but I didn't think Angel understood the severity of it. She was just worried about her mother and couldn't be concerned about anything or anyone else. I totally got that. As we waited, she turned to me and brought her hand to my cheek, causing me to flinch. "You're hurt. Are we gonna go to the hospital?"

I nodded, not wanting to say anything else if I didn't have to. I pulled her hand from my face and gave it a slight squeeze as we heard doors opening. We'd been sitting here for nearly two hours. I was suffering in silence and just ready for this shit to be done. When Tyeis came out, she looked right at us. She smiled slightly as they gave her, her purse. She looked through that shit right there to make sure nothing was missing. I chuckled as I watched.

When she finally got to us, she hugged Angel and said, "I'm okay, sweetheart. I'm sorry I scared you."

It was at this moment that I remembered Angel didn't always process things as well as us. It was evident in this moment. I'd completely forgotten she even had a disability. This situation had thrown her for a loop. Tyeis stared up at me. "I'm sorry, Decaurey. I couldn't let him make it. Although you fucked him up with those body shots, I needed his fucking jaw to be immobile."

"First of all, I can't believe you can hit hard enough to break somebody's jaw. Secondly, what happened back there?"

She smirked, and I supposed that was her response to my statement about her basically being Mike Tyson. "They mostly asked all the same fucking questions they asked at Deanie's, then they were asking about my history with Tyrese. I think Lennox knows something about him or who he's connected to that might be of interest to you. It might be where you think you know him from. Tyrese has family from Beaumont, I think. Although he was born and raised in Houston, his family ties are strong. But enough talking. We need to get you to the hospital. Do you think your jaw is broken?"

I shrugged my shoulders then got on the app to request a Lyft. I was curious as to who this nigga was. Lennox would probably wait until we got back to tell me. Turning to Ty, I said, "Cancel your flights. Y'all can ride back to Beaumont with me. I'm going to need an extra driver since I'll probably be on pain meds."

I had to quit trying to talk. My jaw and face were hurting so fucking bad, I could barely breathe. The paramedic had insisted that I go straight to the hospital, but I couldn't leave Angel and Tyeis on their own. Tyeis grabbed my hand and then used her other hand to gently wipe the side of my mouth. "There was a little blood there. We need to get to the hospital in a hurry. You sound winded."

I only nodded as we walked outside to wait for the Lyft. I was thankful for Lennox's influence; otherwise, Tyeis and I would be sitting in jail, and poor Angel would be left to fend for herself. Within a couple of minutes, the Lyft arrived. As soon as we got in, my phone started ringing. When I saw Storm's number, I rolled my eyes.

"Hello?"

"Uh huh. You can't move your fucking jaw 'cause you out there trying to act like a Henderson. We don't get fucked up though."

I remained quiet, because I didn't even feel like talking to his ass right now. "Na, I'm fucking wit'chu. Lennox told us ol' dude had a few broken bones himself and that Tyeis even delivered a blow. Anyway, when you get back, come holla at all of us at Jasper's barbershop. It's a lot of shit involved in this that we need to talk about."

"Okay."

"Go get that shit fixed. See you tomorrow or the day after. Just let me know."

"I will."

I ended the call as Tyeis stared at me. "They have info about how that dude is connected to us," I said, being careful with my language in the presence of a foreigner. I didn't like saying the word nigga around anyone that wasn't black. I didn't want them to think it was okay for them to use it... or that *I* was okay with them using it. "I have to meet up with everybody when I get back for them to enlighten me."

Tyeis nodded then fidgeted with her nails. "I'm sorry. My involvement with him caused all this mess."

"Naw, don't do that. How would you know you were dealing with a fu—idiot? That ain't on you. It's on him."

I had forgotten that quickly that the lil man was driving. He'd stared at us in his rearview mirror a couple of times already. Bringing my attention back to Ty, I saw she was nodding. "Look at me, baby." When she did so, I continued. "This ain't on you, okay? Besides, this shit may be on the Hendersons. If so, they gon' compensate me for all my pain and suffering."

I leaned back against the seat and rested my jaw. I kept saying that I needed to quit talking, but my ass just kept going, making it worse. "Thank you, Decaurey."

"You ain't gotta thank me. That's what a real man does... protects his woman, regardless of the situation and who started it."

With that, I closed my eyes and tried to concentrate on breathing. Tyeis didn't say anything else. She just gently massaged my chest, doing her best to be there for me emotionally, although I knew she was probably close to falling apart on the inside. I appreciated her efforts. Maybe I was a positive influence on her, like my presence made her better in this moment. I fully expected her to be off the rails because of this shit.

When we got to the hospital, I thanked the driver and helped the ladies out of the car. I pulled up my app to tip him as we went inside to see what they could do for me. When I saw all the fucking people everywhere, I said, "Looks like we should have brought our own bed."

---

I SAT in the passenger seat of my SUV and watched Tyeis adjust the seat and mirrors before she took off. We had a four-hour drive to get to Beaumont. I just wanted to sleep. They gave me some nice pain killers to help with the hairline fracture. Thankfully, I didn't need extensive surgery. Had it been broken, I would probably just be getting out of the hospital or possibly still be there, depending on what the doctor had to say.

They wired my mouth shut, and that shit had me nauseated as hell when I came out of the procedure day before yesterday. The last thing I wanted to have to do while my mouth was wired shut was throw up. I would surely have to get used to drinking protein shakes and liquids all the time, because I would be this way for possibly six weeks.

My sleep had been limited since I practically had to sleep sitting up last night. They told me I needed to sleep that way for at least a week. Hopefully, those pain pills would have me out for the count later. I refused to take one while Tyeis was driving though. I didn't want to be too out of it in case she needed me.

She'd been really nervous so I was glad Angel was here. She was able to keep her mom calm when I couldn't. She'd sat in bed with me at the hospital and had me lay my head against her. It was like she just wanted to take care of me. I appreciated that, but I felt like she probably felt guilty. I didn't want her feeling that way, because it wasn't her fault nor her guilt to bear.

As she drove, she ate a beignet she got from Café Du Monde. I wanted to snatch that shit right out of her hand. This was going to be torture for me. I couldn't eat shit. I supposed Smoothie King would have to be my best friend. As she licked her fingers, she glanced over at me. I was staring right at her, thinking how I wouldn't be able to taste her pussy for nearly two months. I slowly shook my head as I thought about it.

"What's wrong, baby?"

"I feel like you teasing me right now," I said slowly so she would understand what I was saying.

I knew things would get better once the slight discomfort wore off. Then I would be able to talk faster like Kanye and 50 Cent did in the songs they recorded with their jaws wired shut. She glanced at me again as her cheeks reddened. "I'm sorry," she said, then poked her lip out.

I grabbed her hand and squeezed it as she got on the interstate to get us the fuck out of here. They were still holding Tyrese in jail, so we were both happy about that. We knew he would get released at some point though. I was just anxious to find out who he was. He was obviously someone the Hendersons had a problem with.

As if I'd thought them up, my phone started to ring, so I pulled it from my pocket. I grunted a bit because my shoulder was sore as fuck. Thankfully it was only bruised and not broken. That would have been something else I would've had to deal with. When I looked at the caller ID, I saw it was Jasper. "Hello?"

"What's up, street fighter? You done got them knuckles wet, boi!"

I rolled my eyes and chuckled. Jasper could make a joke out of any damn thing. "Man... what's up?"

"I just wanted to know if you were coming today or tomorrow to make up for your haircut appointment. Oh, wait a minute. Y'all are all meeting here today, right?"

"Yeah. This evening. I'm anxious to know who this Tyrese dude is."

"Mm hmm. This shit finna knock your fucking socks off and have you breaking those fucking wires off your jaws like DMX did, nigga."

"It's that bad?"

"Hell yeah. But we gon' talk about that shit later this evening. I'll cut your hair when you get here, so come about thirty minutes before the meeting."

"They say a time? Because Storm ain't said."

"Where are you now?"

"We just left about thirty minutes ago, if that."

"A'ight. Well, it's only nine. The meeting probably won't be until six or so. You got time, nephew. Listen... I'm proud of you for standing up for your woman. Your job is to protect her at all costs. That's one thing that should never fall by the wayside, no matter the situation or how she's behaving. She should always feel safe with you. Love goes without saying. But never be a punk ass nigga, especially when it comes to your family. Her daughter is now your daughter. Although y'all ain't married, you gotta show her that you're worth marrying. You feel me?"

"Absolutely. I appreciate your words of wisdom, Unc. I admire your relationship with your wife. Y'all are goals for real. I know y'all have issues like the next couple, but the way y'all work through shit is admirable."

"I love that woman, and she loves me. Ain't shit more important, so we protect that with our lives. Love gotta shine through every situation. We admit when we're at fault and that's a form of love, man. When people learn that shit, marriages will last so much longer. It's about y'all as a team, but you still have to cater to individual desires and respect each other's opinions and feelings."

"Yeah. You need to put on a class about that shit."

He chuckled. "I gotta go, street fighter. My wife needs big daddy."

"Aww shit. Bye, nigga."

I ended the call while he laughed, then set my phone on the console. "That conversation seemed interesting," Tyeis said.

"Yeah, it was. I can admit that I have flaws. I think Jasper will be a great mentor for me when it comes to relationships. The man understands his woman like you wouldn't believe. I want to be the same way. I think I'm understanding already, but depending on what the future brings, I could need advice."

She nodded. "I get it. I think you're extremely understanding too. I thank God for you and Angel every day. Decaurey, you are everything I need... temper and all."

I chuckled and slowly shook my head. "Yeah, I know I have a bad temper sometimes. I'm impatient as hell, but when I love, I love hard. The only person that can make me stop loving you is you."

It seemed she stopped breathing as my face heated up. She'd

caught what I said... something I said I wouldn't reveal right now. "Decaurey. You love me?"

My face was hot as hell as I shifted in my seat. *Man up, nigga.* I stared at her as she divided her attention between me and the road. "Pull over, baby."

I needed to be able to stare into her eyes while I expressed my love. This shit was insane. We'd only known one another for like four months now and had only been around each other a few times, and I was in love like a sucker ass nigga. Instead of pulling over to the shoulder, she exited the freeway and parked in the lot of a shopping center.

When she turned to me, I could see the glossiness of her eyes. I caressed her hand in mine as I stared at her light pink, pointed nails. When I looked back up at her, a tear had fallen. I released her hand to gently swipe it away, along with the hair that had fallen to her face from her messy bun. "Tyeis, I love you. I didn't want to reveal that so soon to you, because I guess I was trying to protect myself in a way. Obviously, that shit so intense it just fell from my lips. I love you, baby."

She started crying more, and before long, her cries were audible. Angel reached over and rubbed her left shoulder, doing her best to comfort her mother. "Decaurey, no man has said those words and caused this effect. I can feel the love you have for me, and you saying it just confirms that what I feel is real."

She closed her eyes tightly and took a deep breath. "Tyeis, I'm not pressuring you to say it back. I'm a fast mover, and I know that you aren't. Say it when the spirit moves you to do so... when you're sure about the depth of your feelings for me. I ain't going nowhere. I'll be right here whenever you're ready to express yourself. Okay?"

"Thank you for understanding me so much. I've never had that, and I promise, from here on out, I will cherish it like the rarity it is. I'm definitely falling for you, and I promise to let you know as soon as

I hit rock bottom. I feel like I'm not far away from it. Your words have been beautiful."

"You don't have to thank me. A man in love should do his best to understand his woman at all times. There will be things that I won't understand, but it's still my job to work through it the best way I can. You and Angel have a rider for life," I said as I glanced back at her to see the wide smile on her face. "Angel has a *Demon Slayer*, and *Hunter X Hunter* partner in crime for life too."

She giggled then leaned forward and kissed my cheek. I was pretty sure my face was red at that point, especially when she lightly pinched my cheek like I was a little boy and she was an older woman. I chuckled, and Tyeis did as well. I turned my attention back to Tyeis and saw how relaxed her face looked. She normally had a slight frown on her brow. That seemed to be just her natural look, but not now. Her eyebrows were slightly lifted, and she had a closed-mouth smile gracing her beautiful lips.

"I do have to thank you, because there are a lot of men that don't understand that concept. I've never felt so free to be me with anyone, without worrying about how they would perceive me. You don't realize the weight that has lifted from my shoulders."

"I'm glad I could make you lighter. That frees up energy for other things," I responded, then wriggled my eyebrows.

"On that note, we need to get back on the road so I can find out what other things you're speaking of."

Angel rolled her eyes and sat back in her seat, clicking her seat belt back on as I chuckled. I shifted in my seat to face forward, and Tyeis took off with a rare smile on her face.

## CHAPTER SIXTEEN

### TYEIS

"The way that man bore his heart to me was indescribable, Jess. Thank you for the hookup. Decaurey is the one, without a doubt."

"I'm so happy for you, boo."

I frowned slightly. She seemed worried about something. We'd just gotten back to town, and since Jess was in town, we decided to go have a late lunch. Decaurey had tightened me up nicely as soon as we got to his place. He worshipped my body like never before. It seemed every time we connected, it became more intense. I knew his admission had played a huge role in that.

He'd been holding back, trying not to allow me to feel what he felt while making love to me. There were no holds barred today. He kissed every inch of my body and admired it like one of God's perfect gifts. That manly aggressive grace was on ten once we got into it. He had a bitch crying. That was the only way I could express the pleasure I was feeling without scaring the fuck out of my daughter.

Angel had retreated to what she called her room. When Decaurey told her he was building a house and that she would have a permanent room there, she could barely contain her excitement. I could barely contain mine either. He was saying that he planned for us to be a family. That was something I'd always wanted, and I believed my daughter craved it too. To know a man accepted me and all my flaws and accepted my daughter as his own felt amazingly unbelievable.

I took a sip of my tea as I stared at Jess. She started fidgeting under my gaze, so I surely knew something was up. "Jess. Spill it."

She closed her eyes and took a deep breath. "I felt so bad about not telling Nate everything and him finding out at the shoot. I'm in love with Brixton, but I have a soft spot for him. I know it's because we shared our vulnerabilities with one another about our mothers. I just can't seem to let it go. Seeing his emotions through his gaze almost crippled me at the shoot. However, seeing Brixton's insecurity and anger nearly killed me."

"You have an emotional tie to Nate, but you gon' have to find a way to let it go, boo. Why was Brix angry?"

"Just that we were in the position we were in. We got into a huge argument. He was acting like I invited Nate to the shoot. Nate was the reason I even had the shoot to begin with. I told him if he had a problem with that, he needed to reevaluate the part he played in all this with his prideful bullshit he was on that caused me to seek solace in another man in the first damn place."

"Aww shit. Are y'all good now though? That was what? A couple of weeks ago?"

"Not quite two weeks. We aren't arguing, but I can still feel the tension. He doesn't want me talking to Nate anymore and told me had I not been talking to him occasionally, Nate wouldn't still be pining after me. I haven't talked to Nate, except at the shoot, in nearly two months."

"He has a point, Jess. Why did you think you could tell that man that you and Nate slept together and him be okay with y'all being friends? Again, you and Nate have an emotional connection. There's no way y'all can just be friends without something eventually becoming inappropriate. You owe them both an apology, and Brix needs to be listening when you apologize to Nate. What did he say to you at the shoot anyway?"

She swiped away the tears from her face then stared at me. I already knew what that meant. "He loves you, doesn't he?"

"Yeah. He said he hated that things didn't work out between the two of us, but he loved me enough to want me to be happy, even if it wasn't with him. Whether we talked or not, he would always discreetly make sure I was good. After that exchange, I knew I could never be around him again, because all I wanted to do was kiss his lips. What's wrong with me?"

I reached across the table and grabbed her hand. "Jess, monogamy is hard, especially for sexual creatures like me and you, but it isn't impossible. If you love Brix as much as you say you do, this should be easy. I know you're in love with him because you wouldn't have accepted his proposal had you not been. I think I know that much about you. I need you to focus on that love and make things right between you. Assure him that he's all you need. He needs validation, boo."

She nodded. "You're right. I suppose just knowing that I broke Nate's heart got to me. Seeing him again only made that worse. He also said that if I ever did another video for Noah, he wouldn't be there. Had he known I'd told Brix everything, he wouldn't have shown up this time."

"I respect him. He seems like a very mature and wise man. But now I need you to be a very mature, wise woman. You know good and got damn well you wouldn't be cool with Brix talking to a chick he done slept with."

She smiled slightly. "I'd give that ho a Henderson beat down... his ass too. I wouldn't be cool with that shit from jump. He said it was okay at first."

I twisted my lips to the side. "Why would you even have the fucking audacity to ask that man if it was cool? The nerve of you,

Jess. That man was trying to give you what he thought was important to you. But if *I* saw the way Nate looked at you, *I know* he saw that shit. That man was looking like he wanted to tear you apart."

"I know. I'ma fix it. I have to. Losing Brix would kill me, just like losing Decaurey almost did to you, no matter how short a time that separation was. I really am happy for you, boo. You deserve love, and Angel deserves it too. Oh! Did you ever call bitch ass Kelvin?"

"Hell yeah, but that muthafucka ain't answering my calls. He knows that I was going to chew him up one side and down the fucking other. *Nobody* hurts my sweet Angel and gets away with it. That girl doesn't have a hateful bone in her body and was probably excited as hell to talk to him, despite the shit I told her about his ignant ass."

Jess laughed and said, "A'ight, damn. Come back, boo! You went completely left when I brought that nigga up."

"That nigga sours on my fucking stomach like spoiled rice dressing at a cookout."

She laughed even harder. I couldn't even finish eating my flauta at Casa Olé, and I loved their chicken flautas smothered in queso. Their refried beans were good too, but I was about to have to box it. I huffed loudly as Jess laughed more. She always effectively changed the conversation and put the fucking fire under my pot while she turned her burner off.

"Jess, fuck you."

She nearly spit her water out from laughing so hard. I grabbed my phone and called Decaurey. "Hello?"

"Hey, baby. Jess on my fucking nerves, so I need you to calm me down."

She laughed more, and he chuckled. "I got'chu, baby. You need me to kiss you all over your body again? I can't wait until I can lick every inch of you and have your body going into convulsions all from the way my tongue strokes your fat pussy."

I was damn near about to slide out of my chair. Decaurey had my eyes fluttering and everything. "Baby," I practically moaned out. "I said calm me down, not turn me on."

He chuckled as Jess rolled her eyes. "My bad. Did it work though?"

"It did. Now I have to get some of you before you leave to go to Nome. I'm about to box my food up and head there. How's Angel?"

"She's good. She fell asleep while we were watching *Castle In the Sky*."

"Let me guess... Anime."

"Yep."

"Lawd have mercy. That shit ain't nothing but cartoons."

"Hey, na! Hold that shit up. Don't be downing what we watch for entertainment. Ain't nobody say shit when you watching those messy ass reality shows."

I laughed as I listened to him laugh too. I glanced up at Jess to see her watching me with a smile on her beautiful face. "I'll see you when I get there, sandman."

"Mm hmm. I got'cho sandman."

Jess was trying to hold in her laughter because I was sure she didn't want Bestie Jessie to come up. As I was about to end the call, he said, "I love you, baby."

I swore, I nearly burst into tears. Whenever he said it, my eyes watered. He'd said it repeatedly while he made love to me. "Okay, baby," I said softly, then pressed end.

Jess frowned slightly. "What's wrong?"

"Whenever he tells me he loves me, it overwhelms me. It feels like a dream that a man could love me so much."

She smiled at me and grabbed my hand. "I still quiver inside when Brix says it. It never gets old. It's a feeling you'll cherish forever."

"Call him and let me hear you tell him that."

Her eyes widened. Jess held so much inside, and she was always afraid to say how she really felt. She released my hand and hesitantly pulled her phone from her bag. It was like her skin had gotten clammy and her breathing pattern had changed. Once she brought the phone to her ear, I grabbed her trembling hand.

"Hey, Brix... I just wanted to say that I love you. I still quiver inside when you tell me you love me. I'll cherish that feeling for the rest of my life... Yes. I have goosebumps..."

She wasn't lying. I could see them appearing on her arm. "I'm so sorry, Brix. I love you so much, and I don't ever want you to feel that anyone else is more important than you. When it comes to you, no one else matters. You're my world, baby."

I watched the tears fall down her cheeks then stood and walked around the table to sit next to her. I wrapped my arms around her as she continued to talk to him. "I know... I promise to never make you feel that way again. You have my word... I'll be there shortly, baby... Okay. I love you too."

She ended the call and remained in my arms. Her arms wrapped around my waist after she set her phone on the table. "Thank you, Ty. I needed that. You're always there for me. I love you, girl."

"I love you more. You're the only friend I have, and I'll go to war for your stubborn, crazy ass."

She giggled. "Ditto, bitch."

I laughed and pushed her away from me. Her tears affected me so much. She had me sitting here crying with her ass. "Let's get our asses out of here and get to our men. Is Brix meeting with them later?"

"Yeah. He knows nothing, so I'm not sure why they want him there."

"Do you know?"

"Yeah, I know, but I've been told to keep my fucking mouth shut. Uncle Storm's words exactly," she said as she rolled her eyes.

"Damn. This must really be serious."

"It is. I'll tell you tomorrow. When are you and Angel leaving?"

"Day after tomorrow, but only to get more clothes. I gotta make sure my baby is taken care of."

"Decaurey ass ain't cripple," she said with a dismissive wave.

"You gon' get off my sandman though. He was protecting me and Angel."

"I told you his ass can't fight."

I laughed. "Don't do my baby. He fucked Tyrese up. I can say confidently that I feel safe when he's with me."

She smiled softly. "That's what's up, boo. We have good men."

"That we do. Now let's go take care of their babified asses."

## CHAPTER SEVENTEEN

### DECAUREY

"I know y'all fucking lying."
 I was outdone and pacing back and forth. I'd heard stories about that nigga and how much hell he'd given the Hendersons. I was around for some of it. "When he started fucking with Marcus, we knew we had to put a stop to that shit. Kenny made sure the job was complete, because out of everyone here, he fucked his life up the most. It's still a miracle to me how he and Keisha made it through that," Jasper said.

They were speaking of Reggie. He was a police officer that gave them hell. He was friends with Uncle Kenny in school and dated Aunt Tiffany at one time. Then the nigga manipulated and fucked Aunt Keisha, harassed Aunt Jenahra about the death of her ex-husband, harassed my dad about said death, stalked Aunt Syn, and tried to blackmail Uncle Marcus. That muthafucka had to go ASAP.

When Storm and Jasper got the best of him, that nigga only became more conniving. They'd already fucked him up after they learned of him setting Uncle Kenny and his wife up, all because he was jealous of him. The nigga just didn't learn. When Pop tried to kill himself was when Storm and Jasper worked his ass over. He'd made the comment that it was one less Henderson for him to worry about while Pop was on the floor, bleeding everywhere.

He and Storm had another run in when that nigga was after Syn before she and Marcus got married. Marcus knew people that would grab that nigga and fuck him up. Everybody wanted his ass gone because it seemed nothing was being done about his ass. He was fired from the sheriff's office, but then still became a city cop. When they got there to see if the job had been done, Uncle Kenny checked his pulse, only to see he was still alive. He broke that nigga's neck right there in front of everybody.

"I wish we were lying, nephew. We have to watch his ass closely. Him being Reggie's nephew could mean he's out for revenge. That was why you recognized his ass. He looks just like Reggie," Uncle Kenny said.

I was still pacing. When I learned of what he had said about Pop, I wanted to get at him, and I didn't even know his ass back then. I never really knew him, but I definitely had extensive knowledge of who he was now. I was happy I didn't take my anger with the situation out on Tyeis. This shit had nothing to do with her. Had I let my temper get the best of me, she would be back in Houston, and we wouldn't be together.

"So what are we going to do?" I asked as Marcus ran his hand over his beard.

"We gotta be careful so these white folks don't shove me and Marcus right out of office. The election is next month. They don't need to know some real niggas finna be running Big City Nome," Storm said, causing damn near everybody to roll their eyes.

"I got it," Philly said, surprising everybody.

Philly worked for the family business. He was the only non-relative, besides my recent contract, that worked for the family. While they considered us family, we weren't blood related. Philly was Tiffany's husband's brother. He was also the first cousin of family friend, Legend Semien. Philly had left the game behind years ago and had done some time in prison... just a year or so.

When he saw everyone staring at him, including his own brother, Ryder, he said, "This will scratch the itch I've been having."

"I don't want you to get caught up again, bruh. You have way more to lose now. Kema, the twins, and Kiana," Ryder said.

"I'll help him," Kenny said, volunteering.

"I'll help too," I said, surprising my damn self. "I have a reason to want to take his ass out. Stalking my fucking woman like he don't value his life."

"Unfortunately, I have to steer clear of this, so does Jakari, Storm, and Marcus, but y'all know we got y'all back with whatever y'all wanna do," Pop said.

He and Jakari were the ones in the public eye the most for the family business. Nesha was too, but of course, she would have nothing to do with this. "So are we gonna watch him or just go straight for the fucking jugular?" Brixton asked.

"Once he gets out, we'll watch him for a couple of weeks to see if he's up to something. If he is, most likely he'll make a move by then. I don't know why people always tryna fuck with us. He should know better. They didn't even have a fucking body for Reggie's funeral. He gon' learn though when those hogs get to his ass," Kenny said.

I frowned. "Hogs?"

When they noticed the confusion on my face, they all chuckled. "Wild hogs will eat yo' ass... bones and all. We would only have to bury the teeth and hair. Does Tyrese have a lot of hair?" Jasper asked.

"Naw. He bald headed like the singer," I responded.

He nodded. "Spread something sweet on his body, and he's gone without a trace. I feel like he gon' do some shit to get fucked up. I just hate that it has to come to this. The Hendersons are powerful as fuck now. Why would he think he can take us on by himself?" Jasper said.

"All I know is he don't need to start talking and putting our names on people's minds. It was only our status that kept us in the clear about Reggie. People witnessed our disdain for his ass, especially when Jen went through the ringer," Pop added. "We should have been prime suspects, especially Storm and Jasper, because they got cuffed for beating the fuck out of him."

"W.J., I did get questioned," Storm spoke up.

Everyone turned to him stunned. "Right after?"

"A few days later. I told them to go fuck themselves. They had nothing tying me to it, so it wasn't like they could arrest me."

"Jasper, did they question you?" Pop asked, turning his attention to him.

"Yeah. Same day they questioned Storm. You were doing well with the business and shit. You didn't need to be worried about that. Besides, that shit wasn't relevant. Hell, honestly, I'd forgotten all about it."

"Shit. Well, y'all gon' have to really be careful. Maybe we need to contract it out."

"W.J., come on na. You know I can go undetected," Philly said.

I'd heard that nigga killed somebody in a Taco Bell drive-thru without getting caught. How the hell did somebody get away with some shit like that? Philly used to be a kingpin, and from what Malachi had said, the nigga was ruthless. His body count was enumerable. Philly didn't even remember how many people had succumbed to his authority.

Everyone turned to Pop to see what his response would be. Kenny added, "I won't let him be reckless, man. Like Ryder said, he has more to lose now, so I don't even think we have that to worry about. You know I'm sneaky as fuck. The most conniving FBI agent won't be able to find evidence. They can suspect all day long. It won't get them anywhere."

Pop nodded repeatedly. "A'ight. Who's gonna keep watch?"

"I will," Brix said, stepping up.

"I will too," Jakari said.

I was hoping he would. Jakari was extremely smart and resourceful. Not saying that Brix wasn't, but I knew Jakari's skills better than I knew Brix's. I wished Lennox could help us, although I knew why he couldn't. Him being a detective could get us all kinds of insight. However, with people knowing he was associated with the Henderson family, if we ever became suspects, they would be digging in all his shit first. One slipup would implicate the entire family.

Pop nodded his head again. He turned to me and said, "I'm sorry the sins of our past got you involved in this bullshit, son. We got your back though. Don't worry about shit. I like how you handled your job of protecting your woman. Your mama was worried but proud at the same time. I wasn't worried. I knew you would be able to handle your own if you were pushed."

I frowned slightly as Jasper chuckled. "What you mean if I were pushed?"

Storm laughed, and it caused everyone else to laugh. "Nigga, you was a friendly fat boy that nobody took seriously. Ol' soft ass."

I shoved Storm, causing him to nearly fall over as he laughed. "Aye, nigga! Keep your hands to yourself. Fucking up Tyrese done gave yo' ass too much confidence. I'm gon' bring that ego right back the fuck down. Fuck a hairline fracture. I'm gon' shatter that shit."

I huffed as I rolled my eyes. They continued laughing at my expense. As a fat boy, I'd gotten into plenty fights in school, trying to prove I wasn't a pushover. People thought because I was friendly and funny that I wouldn't fight or that I would get fucked up in a fight. It was my fault why Tyrese even got that lick in. I'd taken my eyes off him for a split second, to make sure Tyeis and Angel were out the way, when he caught me slipping.

"Well, we got shit to do. Brix and Jakari, y'all will report to Philly or Kenny. Philly and Kenny, keep the rest of us in the loop. I'm gon' talk to my son-in-law about what's going on, just in case we need him on the other side."

He was talking about Lennox. He stood from his seat and approached me. "Let me talk to you, son."

I nodded and stood as well, following him outside to his pickup truck. He turned to me once he got to his door. "Your guys are doing extremely well, and Chas has approved the contract Nesha drew up. I'm proud of you."

That was the last thing I was expecting. I thought he wanted to talk about that bullshit we just finished talking about. "Thanks, Pop. Although you've only been in my life for about seven years or so, I've learned a lot about business from you. I appreciate you taking my grown ass in as your son."

He gave me a one-sided smile and pulled me in for a hug. "You're the son I always wanted. God gave me three girls, and that's probably a good thing. I would've raised a boy in all my brokenness to be just like I was. You met me at a time where I was willing to live in my truth and become a better man. It was perfect timing."

He released me, and before he could get in his truck, his phone was ringing. "That's probably your mama. She said she would warm my dinner when I was on my way if I called."

He pulled the phone from his pocket and frowned slightly. He brought the phone to his ear and answered. "Hey, Dad."

I saw his facial expression soften and his eyebrows lift in concern as Uncle Kenny came running out of the barbershop. "Okay. We're on our way."

"I have to get to Mom and Dad's house. You coming?"

"Yeah."

I hopped in the truck with him, knowing that this couldn't be good with the way Kenny peeled out. "What's going on?" I asked after he backed out of his parking spot.

"Mama is unresponsive."

*Grandma Henderson.* I lowered my head as he sped to their place. "Is she breathing?" I asked.

"Yeah. She has a pulse, but he can't wake her up."

I sent a text to my mama because I didn't think he had. She needed to be here for him. While I knew his past with his parents wasn't the greatest, they were all in a great place now. When we got there, Kenny was flying in the driveway right behind us, along with everyone else. When Pop parked, he remained still. He didn't try to hop out the truck or anything.

"You okay, Pop?"

"Yeah, but Kenny needs to go in first. I don't want to be in his way."

I frowned slightly as I watched everyone else run in except Storm. He came over to the driver's side of the truck and opened the door. He didn't say a word. There were no tears or even the slightest panic in either of their demeanors. "Come on, bruh," Storm said.

He extended his hand to Pop, and he grabbed it and got out of the truck. My mama drove up right after since they only lived a couple of minutes away. I sent Tyeis a message. She was at my place without transportation. *Baby, I'm gonna be late getting back. Grandma Henderson is unresponsive. We just got here and are about to go in to see what's going on.*

She responded immediately. *Oh no! I'm so sorry. I can't be there for you! How am I gonna get there?*

*Don't panic, baby. It's okay. I'll be there as soon as I can. We have to come to Beaumont to get her to a hospital. I can pick you up if you want to be with me.*

*Yes, please.*

I followed Storm and Pop through the door to see everyone kind of standing around. They all looked nervous. Tiffany approached Pop and said, "She's awake, but she's asking for you."

It was like he knew she would be. As I went toward the couch to sit next to Nesha and Jess, he said, "Decaurey, come with me, please."

I nodded and followed him to the back of the house into my grandparents' bedroom. I wasn't sure why he wanted me to go with him instead of my mama or one of his siblings, but I went along. When we walked into the room, Grandpa Henderson was lying next to her in the bed, but as soon as he saw my dad, he got up and allowed him to come to the bed. She stared up at him then patted the bed for him to join her.

After he got in bed with her, he wrapped her in his arms, and she laid her head on his shoulder. Grandpa offered me a seat next to the bed. As I sat, I heard her say in a soft voice, "You were my first love, son."

That alone wasn't a great sign. Grandma Henderson was loud as hell all the time until lately when her health started failing her, but it was even softer in this moment. "Mama, why aren't you allowing Kenny to take you to the hospital?" Pop asked.

"Shhh. I needed to talk to you, baby. When I found out I was pregnant, I was so happy. When King said he wanted no parts of raising a kid, I was devastated. But you were who kept me from falling into a full depression. I knew I had to stay healthy for you. Even still, I was dehydrated, and my blood pressure kept dropping because they said I wasn't eating and drinking enough. When you came out so strong, with amazing vitals, I knew you would be a strong man."

She brought her hand to his cheek and stared into his eyes. "You could have disowned me a long time ago, especially when you found out the truth. I didn't behave like a mother who loved her child, but you never turned your back on me... on us. You were willing to eliminate yourself before causing harm to us. You shouldn't have been in a predicament to where that would even have to be... a decision," she said, trying to catch her breath.

"Mama, let Kenny take you to the hospital."

She shook her head. "I'm tired, baby. Life has been hard, and I made it harder on myself sometimes. You have become an amazing man that your son and daughters can respect and love. I'm so proud of you, W.J. Get your sisters and brothers in here... Marcus too. Get my grandbabies."

I wasn't sure why she specifically said Marcus too, but I supposed I was about to find out. I knew she wasn't his biological mother, so maybe there was some shit she needed to get off her conscience with him… or at least words of love.

When everyone came in, I backed away so they could get close. Her kids, along with Marcus all surrounded the bed. She looked at all of them one by one. "Jen, you are so beautiful. My first daughter. You had the weight of responsibility on your shoulders, and I'm sorry, baby. I was so happy when you found true happiness so you could stop pretending to be okay. Chrissy, I'm proud of you, too, for letting Avery's sins not become your own and moving… on with your life."

She took a couple of deep breaths then brought her gaze to Uncle Kenny. "I always knew you would be knowledgeable in all areas. You were that way as a kid. I'm proud of you, son. You went through the fire and came out as pure gold. Jasper, my favorite weed smoker." She smiled, and he chuckled as he wiped a lone tear that had fallen from his eye. "The way you love your wife speaks volumes. You love her even when everyone condemns you for it. Never change that. Make sure she's always confident in your love. It's beautiful."

She coughed a bit then took some deep breaths. She was laboring, and I knew it wouldn't be long. "Tiff, my rodeo queen. You didn't have a choice but to be tough. Those boys gave you the blues growing up. I'm proud of you too, baby. You didn't let being a woman keep you from accomplishing great things that not even some men could accomplish. It's still hard to believe that my baby is a trendsetter and will be in rodeo history, being studied by kids all over the world."

I glanced over at Storm to see his red face. He wasn't crying, but I could tell he was on the verge. Tiff was in Ryder's arms, crying her eyes out. Aunt Jenahra and Aunt Chrissy were doing the same with their spouses. "Seven, I knew your bad ass would always be a bad ass. Now you have five bad asses of your own. I thought your mean butt would be single for a long time. What I love about you, of course besides the fact that you were my baby boy, was that there was no guesswork required. You were always a straight shooter and about your business. Nome couldn't ask for a better mayor. I'm so proud."

She took more deep breaths as the siblings and their spouses embraced one another. When she turned to Marcus, she extended her hand. His eyebrows lifted, and he went closer to her. He put his hand in hers. "I know I played a horrible role in your childhood. I'm so sorry. I know I've apologized before, but I also wanted to let you know, son, that I'm proud of you. You completely turned your life around. Despite your father giving you everything you deserved, you could have kept the same mindset. You didn't do that."

She coughed a couple of times, then Grandpa put a straw to her lips for her to sip some water. She nodded, I supposed thanking him. "Marcus, you are an amazing father. Your children adore you. When you became the custodial parent for Malia, I saw a change in you that nearly made me cry. In that moment, I felt like I was a part of your progression. I was beyond happy to witness you maturing overnight and getting the help you needed to become a better man for your children and for Syn."

Marcus nodded as she released his hand. "My grandbabies, Grandma loves y'all. Always remember that. Nesha, I'm sorry I probably won't be here to see my first great grandbaby. You will be an amazing mother, because you are an amazing daughter and granddaughter. Jess, I'm gonna miss the wedding, but I'll be there in spirit. Jakari, the business is gonna be yours. Make me proud. I'll be watching. Decaurey, congratulations on your contract, baby. I'm proud of you."

Only her older adult grandchildren were here. I supposed the others probably didn't know. I glanced at Pop as Mama wrapped her arms around his waist. It was completely quiet until Grandma said, "Y'all go home. I love all of you. Wesley will take care of me. He'll call y'all if he needs to."

We all started leaving the room one at a time after kissing her head or cheek. When we got to the front room, everyone found a seat. No one was going home. I was more than sure everyone else would be arriving soon. I walked over to my parents. "Can I use a vehicle to go pick up Tyeis and Angel? My SUV is still at the barbershop."

"I'll take you to get it. I'm the last one in the driveway."

I turned to see Jakari grabbing his keys from the countertop. Seeing the tears on everyone's faces and them being consoled by the ones they loved only made me long for Tyeis. I had to get to her ASAP.

## CHAPTER EIGHTEEN

### TYEIS

As soon as Decaurey walked through the door, I ran to his arms and hugged him tightly. I could tell he was weary and sad. "Are we going to the hospital? They are usually cold, so I can get a sweater."

"No. We're going back to Nome. Angel ready?"

I nodded then went to get her. I wasn't sure why we were going to Nome other than that she may have died already. I didn't ask any questions. I just wanted to be there for him. When Angel and I got back up front, she hugged him tightly, and he kissed the top of her head. He walked toward the door, and we followed him. After locking up, he walked to the SUV and opened our doors for us to get in. Even in this moment, he didn't forsake being a gentleman.

Once he got in, I said, "I don't mind driving."

"I'm okay right now. Maybe on the way home?"

"Okay. However you need me, I'm here."

He nodded and backed out, heading to Nome. I grabbed his hand and held it for the twenty-minute ride there, occasionally lifting it to kiss it. The ride was extremely quiet. He didn't even have music playing, and that was rare. Thankfully, I'd filled Angel in about what was going on so she wouldn't ask a bunch of questions. I knew Decaurey probably just needed peace right now.

Once we got to Nome, cars were everywhere. He drove in the driveway and had to park in the pasture in front of their house. Thankfully, the ground was dry because Southeast Texas hadn't been getting much rain... for the past few months it seemed. He opened our doors and led us down the long driveway toward the front door. I could smell weed the closer we got. They were probably all smoking at this point. I definitely understood the need to.

As we neared the door, I could clearly make out Jasper, Kenny, and Tiffany standing there, passing a blunt. I swore this damn driveway was a mile long. With as big as their family was, there was a need for it. Cars were all over the place. When we got to the door, I noticed Mr. W.J., Jen, and Chrissy were smoking as well. I supposed Storm was avoiding it, still worried about his campaign and not wanting to risk anyone seeing him smoking it.

I spoke to everyone, but I didn't bother introducing Angel. Everyone seemed miles away, and I could totally understand that. I only introduced her to Mrs. Olivia, Decaurey's mother. She hugged Angel so tightly, but I could tell that my daughter felt welcomed by her relaxed demeanor. Once we entered the house, I immediately laid eyes on Jess. I looked up at Decaurey, and before I could say anything, he said, "Go ahead."

I walked over to Jess and sat next to her and hugged her tightly. Finally, she said, "Damn, bitch! You tryna kill me? You about to squeeze all the damn air out of me."

Everyone in earshot started laughing. I took a deep breath and relaxed. They were being themselves. They didn't seem to be as sad as Decaurey was. I had a feeling of why though. His mom's parents were deceased, and he didn't really know his dad's family. So, Grandma Henderson was the only grandparent he had a relationship with. He'd only gotten seven or eight years with her.

"I'm sorry, heifer. I was just tryna console yo' ass. Where's Nesha?"

Jess chuckled. "She's in the bathroom."

I nodded as she hugged Angel then introduced her to Brixton. After Angel sat next to her, I went toward the kitchen to search for Decaurey. He'd grabbed a bottle of water from the fridge and that made me remember I'd packed him a protein shake. I pulled it from my bag, and he smiled at me. "Thank you, baby. I'm fucking starving."

"I figured you would be. You haven't drunk one since earlier, and it's not like you can eat anything."

He practically snatched it from me. "Is your grandpa in the room with your grandma?"

"Yeah. She told everyone to go home, but she had to know that no one would listen."

"So what's going on?"

"She's ready to go and is refusing to go to the hospital. She said she's tired. Other than her having blood pressure issues, I'm not sure if anything else is going on that could have caused this steady decline she's been on."

I gently rubbed circles on his back as he talked. After opening his shake, he started drinking it and nearly got choked. "Slow down, baby. We should have stopped and got you a smoothie too."

"Right. I'm sure they're closed now."

I nodded and glanced at all the food on the countertop and realized Mrs. Jen and Mrs. Chrissy were probably about to cook for everyone. After Decaurey finished his shake, we made our way back out front with everyone else. They were all talking and there was some laughter. All the ones that had been outside had come back in, and children were everywhere. Angel's eyes were wide as she stared at everyone.

She loved children and was probably dying to talk to them. As she sat there, Marcus's daughter grabbed her hand and said, "You ought to come sit with us."

She smiled big and followed the little girl's lead, but when I saw her eyes land on one of Decaurey's male cousins, I frowned slightly. When he noticed her staring at him, he smiled and gave her a head nod. I was so hoping he wouldn't be rude to her. She grinned and her dark skin had a red tint. She was crushing on him. *Lawd Jesus.*

When he got up and sat next to Jakari, I realized that he was probably his brother. They looked a lot alike. If I remembered correctly, both his brothers were grown, grown and too old for my baby. I was pretty sure this guy was at least twenty-four or twenty-five years old. Angel's tender age of eighteen was no match for the freak shit someone that age could expose her to. Then again, someone her age could expose her to all sorts of shit.

I watched her go sit with the other girls, who looked to be teenagers, and they introduced themselves to her. When I saw her turn and point at me, I knew she was telling them that I was her mother. I politely waved at the girls, and they waved back. "So, Angel is making friends, huh?"

I looked up to see Decaurey standing over me. "Yeah. I'm happy about that. But who is that sitting next to Jakari?"

He lifted his head and looked over where they were. "That's his youngest brother, Rylan. Why?"

"Angel was staring at him."

Decaurey smiled and sat next to me as I stared at the brown-skinned cutie. At least she had good taste. He didn't look the least bit country. He wore skinny jeans and a T-shirt, had diamond studs in his ears, a couple of chains around his neck, and J's on his feet. "He may be a little too advanced for baby girl," Decaurey said.

"My thoughts exactly. How old is he?"

"I think he's twenty-five."

"Yeah, that's what I thought. Baby girl gon' have to find someone else who sparks her interest."

Decaurey chuckled and grabbed my hand. I turned to him and used my other hand to stroke his beard. The way he stared at me had my entire body heating up. "Thank you for being here. Although she isn't my biological grandmother, she feels like one, especially since I didn't know my paternal grandparents. I feel like I haven't had enough time with her."

I knew he was probably feeling that way. I just continued to caress his cheek until he pulled my hand away and kissed it. "I understand, and you don't have to thank me for being here for you. I have to admit, I could feel myself getting worked up earlier."

"I could tell by your voice."

"The way you can calm me is scary. No one, besides Angel and Shylou, has been able to do that."

"It's because you can feel my love for you. Not to bring up old shit, but that was why I was so upset with you lying and keeping it from me. I knew I could help you if you allowed me to, baby."

I nodded and trained my gaze on my nails for a moment. Changing the subject, I asked, "So how did the meeting go?"

I'd been dying to ask that question, but no time seemed like the right time. Decaurey took a deep breath. "His attack on me had nothing to do with you, but everything to do with the Hendersons. His uncle gave them a hard ass time for years, and now, I guess he believes it's his turn."

I frowned. The Hendersons must have gotten the best of his uncle for him to think it was his turn. Was this about revenge for something? I supposed Decaurey could see my confusion, because he said, "It would take a lot of time to explain, so I'll tell you later."

"Okay."

"We heard you got your ass whupped."

I frowned and looked up to see the twins... Storm's bad ass mini-mes. "Man, gone somewhere with that shit. Y'all mama know y'all curse?"

They smirked at him, then the bigger one said, "Our dad knows, and that's all that matters. Yo' mouth wired shut so the rumor must be true."

I turned away because I didn't want them to see my smile. Everyone around here, especially Storm and his kids, loved giving Decaurey a hard time. "I told y'all to gone somewhere. Get out my face 'fore I whup y'all's bad asses."

Their eyebrows went up and they crossed their arms over their chest simultaneously. Before they could say another word, Storm said, "Y'all leave that nigga alone. He sensitive right now."

Decaurey slowly shook his head as I put my arm around him. "I swear they work my nerves."

"Then why are you smiling?" I asked him.

"Because I wouldn't have it any other way."

I chuckled as Mr. Henderson came from the back room. Everyone stood as they watched him. When he dropped to the floor crying, we all knew the inevitable had happened. Tiffany ran to him and joined him on the floor, along with Chrissy. Kenny went to the bedroom, and Jenahra gathered all the kids to go to another room in the house. Mr. W.J. immediately got on his phone and called someone.

"I'm so sorry, baby," I said to Decaurey and pulled him close to me.

He wasn't crying audibly, but I could feel his tears against my neck. The cries from everyone else filled the room though. They weren't loud, but because there were so many of them, it was easy to hear. I glanced over at Storm, and when I saw his tears, it moved me as well. He was the hardest of everyone. I didn't know Mrs. Henderson well, but I could clearly tell she was loved by her family.

There wasn't a dry eye in the place as Kenny came from the room, his face and eyes both red and his hair wild. I frowned slightly, because his hair was in a man bun when he went back there. "What happened, Kenny?" Jasper asked.

"She wasn't gone yet. She opened her eyes when I walked in, like she knew it was me. When I sat beside her, she pulled my hair loose and whispered, *'In the jungle the mighty jungle the lion sleeps tonight.'* Then she said she was going to be with Kendrick and babysit him all day. I fell apart. When I looked back up at her, she was gone."

I was confused by what he said, but it was obviously something specific to him. Jasper walked over and hugged him. Watching him break down as his wife, Keisha, joined them broke me too. I didn't even know anyone well enough to be crying this way, but I couldn't help it. I was always extremely empathetic, and so was my daughter. Hopefully, she was in there with Mrs. Jenahra and the kids, comforting them as best she could.

I wrapped my arms around Decaurey tighter as he said, "Kendrick was his son with another woman. The mother killed him when he was only a year old or so. His son loved to play in his hair, so that was probably why she pulled it loose. That was years ago, but I can see how this moment would affect him this way. I can assume that you could never fully get over losing one of your children. You just go on and do your best to live your life without them."

I only cried harder at that revelation. If something ever happened to Angel, it would kill me, and I would never be the same. Kenny was strong, and apparently, the child's death had taken a toll on his wife as well, because instead of her consoling him, he had begun consoling her. This was hard for me, so I could imagine how everyone else was feeling. I wiped my face and lifted my head to look for my girl Jess.

She was in Brixton's arms with her eyes closed. She wasn't crying though. Jess was always hard like Storm, but even he had released tears. I supposed relation was relevant. Had it been her mother, I felt like she wouldn't have been able to keep it together. When Mrs. Jenahra came out of the room with the kids, she said, "Come on, everybody."

It was like they all knew what she wanted, because they all stood and formed a circle. Decaurey and I joined in. Mr. Henderson was barely holding up though. "Daddy, sit on the couch, and we will all surround you."

When he did, Storm's twins sat on either side of him with their arms wrapped around their grandpa. We all surrounded them, and Mrs. Jenahra began by saying, "God is still good. Mama lived a full life of over eighty years. She's resting now."

She bowed her head, and everyone joined her. "Thank you, Lord, for blessing us with the time we had with Mama. Your timing is perfect, and no matter how hard it is or how much it hurts, we will still believe that You are in control. Keep us as we deal with the aftermath of her passing. Be our comfort, strength, and direction. Help us to lean on You even more. Keep our father in Your care. He needs You more now than ever before. In Your son's name, amen."

"Amen," everyone mumbled.

I wrapped my arms around Decaurey as Mrs. Jen and Mrs. Chrissy retreated to the kitchen, and everyone else sat. He lightly kissed my head and said in my ear, "I need to be alone with you, Tyeis."

I stared up at him and nodded. "Let me tell Angel that we are leaving for a little bit."

He nodded and pulled away from me. I found my way to the room they were in, to see all the girls sitting around her in like a campfire circle as she talked. When they noticed me, they all looked up at me. I could see the tears on their faces, and I realized she was probably consoling them. I gave them a tight smile and said, "Angel, Decaurey and I are about to leave for an hour or so. Will you be okay staying here?"

"Please don't leave," Storm's daughter said as she wrapped her arms around Angel.

I couldn't remember her name, but she definitely defied the odds by being so sweet. Angel smiled and hugged her back. "I'll be okay, Mama. Take your time."

I walked over to her and kissed her head and walked out to find

Decaurey hugging Nesha. His hand was on her stomach, and he was rubbing it in a circular motion. I noticed everyone that had hugged her tonight had done that, I supposed trying to keep her calm and reminding her of why she needed to stay as calm as possible.

He looked up at me and kissed the top of Nesha's head. "I gotta go, sis. I'll be back though."

She nodded as she pulled away from him. Once he stood, he pulled his keys from his pocket and handed them to me. I grabbed his hand, and he led me to his Tahoe. "Where do you want me to go, baby?" I asked.

"To my place."

I nodded, knowing exactly what he needed from me: the ultimate display of love that I could give him.

## CHAPTER NINETEEN

### DECAUREY

When we walked through the door of my place, I gently backed Tyeis to the door and began sliding her wide-neck shirt over her shoulders. Her breathing was steady, and it was causing mine to be as well. I was feeling extremely emotional, and I needed her to level me out. There was no other place I would rather pour my emotions than inside of her. I swiftly turned her around to face the door and unclasped her bra.

Just as swiftly as before, I turned her back to me and lightly pinched her nipples. This wire was fucking with me because I wanted to tongue kiss her so bad. I went to her neck instead and placed soft kisses all over it as my hands traveled to the waistband of her jeans then to her ass. Tyeis had ass for days, and I loved squeezing that shit. As I squeezed, I could feel her hands slide between us and unfasten her pants.

I slowly pulled away from her and pulled them off. Going to my knees to pull them off her feet, I placed my nose right in her mound and groaned, since she wasn't wearing underwear. I wanted to taste her pussy. I kissed it and slightly pushed her against the door where she would be leaning enough for me to get to it. I brought my lips to her clit and pulled it between my lips. There was no opening my mouth to catch all her juices, so that shit was all over my chin and rolling down my neck.

Her hands made their way to the back of my head as she lifted one leg to my shoulder. When her hips started to roll, I knew what needed to be done. I stood and yanked her to me, lifting her in my arms, her titties right in my face, and walked to my bedroom. After placing her on her feet, I sat on the bed then scooted to the center and lay on my back. "Come drown me with that pussy, girl."

She wasted no time climbing in the bed and straddling my face. My eyes rolled to the back of my head as she rubbed her pussy up and down my face. This shit had my dick ready to blast off. I lifted my hips and pulled my pants and boxer briefs off and started stroking my dick as her juices traveled all over my face and neck. "Shit!"

Tyeis looked down at me as she slowed her movements. "Everything okay, baby?" she asked breathlessly.

"Hell yeah. Fuck my face to yo' satisfaction."

That was all I had to say for her to go to the fucking theme park. She was dipping, swerving, and twerking that shit on my face as I smacked her ass for encouragement. I swore her juices had run up my nose and got in my fucking eyes, but I refused to make her stop until her cream had played connect the dots with the freckles on my face. "Decaurey, oh my God, baby! Shit!"

She was screaming at the top of her lungs, and that shit turned me on so much, I blasted my seed all over her back. "Fuck!"

Her movements slowed, and she fell off my face to the side of me as her body trembled against mine. I couldn't hardly see a fucking thing, but I still rolled on top of her, letting all her juices fall to her chest and face. Once I pushed inside of her, she moaned loudly. I brought my lips to hers and kissed her softly. When I pulled away, she pulled me back to her and licked my fucking eyes.

I was trying to make love to her, but she was going to have me tearing her fucking ovaries up in a minute. She slowly licked my eyes as I dug my fingertips in her hips, trying to stay at a medium pace. My eyes were slightly burning, and my vision was a little cloudy, but it was better than what it was. I stared into her eyes as she wrapped her legs around my waist, throwing her pussy back at me.

"Damn, Tyeis. I love you, baby. I love you so fucking much."

My strokes went deeper as she dug her nails into my back. Like me, I felt like she was holding back how she really felt. She was trying to be sure. However, while she was evaluating her feelings, I promised myself that I would expose every nerve of my body to show her just how deeply I felt for her. I wanted her to be secure in my feelings for her. After waiting all this time to fall for another woman, I knew I was beyond ready—emotionally, mentally, and spiritually.

Her pussy was so damn hot, it was threatening to take me out the game before I was ready. Her walls always embraced me like a fucking electric blanket in the winter. Going back out in the cold wasn't even a thought, literally or figuratively. I'd stay in her love all day if I could. Just like she said she could feel my love for her before I said it, I could feel her love for me. The way she fought for me and refused to just let me be, told me how much she loved me already.

She wrapped her arms around my neck as her eyes rolled to the back of her head. As if she wasn't wet enough, she squirted. I pulled out of her, and that shit squirted on my abdomen. I swore my dick grew an inch every time she did that. I dived right back inside of her as she arched her back. I pinched her nipple with one hand and gripped her neck with the other then began fucking the shit out of her.

"Ty, fuck! I love this hot, juicy shit."

"And I love your thick, long diiiiick!" she said loudly, then screamed as another orgasm hit her.

Feeling her walls clench me was about to have me nutting all over her cervix. Knowing she was on birth control was like a gift from God. There was no way I wanted to shield myself from everything her pussy had to offer me. I pushed her legs up and looked at the beautiful mess she'd made then lay on top of her. Her legs wrapped around me once again, but I quickly grabbed one and pushed it to her shoulder.

Lying against her, skin-to-skin, was one of the most amazing feelings in the world. Feeling her hard nipples sliding against my chest with every stroke only turned me on even more. I buried my head in the pillow, my mouth close to her ear. "Ty, please don't ever leave me. Promise me that we will always do our best to work out any issues we may have."

She turned her head and kissed my neck, probably realizing that my sensitivity was speaking now. She blew her breath against my neck, and it caused every hair on my body to stand. "You have all of me, Decaurey. Forever, baby. I love you."

I closed my eyes and thrusted balls deep into her and just held my position. Her nails had dug into me even more as she screamed, "Fuck! I love you!"

I lifted my head to stare at her to see the tears cascading down her face. I kissed every one that dropped. "Thank you for trusting me with your heart, baby."

"I trust you with my soul, Decaurey."

I began stroking her again, giving her everything I had to offer. She was mine and always would be. I released my nut within her depths as I rested my forehead on hers. Closing my eyes, I knew that we would only get better from here. I couldn't wait to experience life again with a family this time.

My face felt frozen in place from all her dried juices on it. After I pulled out of her, I said, "We have to take a shower before we go back. I can't even smile right now, girl. Your shit got my face cemented in place."

She laughed so hard as she slapped my arm. She tucked her bottom lip into her mouth as she stared at me. "Well, give me something to put on my face. I'm sure it works wonders for the skin. Your shit gon' be glowing when you wash that deep conditioning mask off."

"Fuck, girl." I went to my knees and rested my dick in my hand. "Come get this shit then."

She lay in front of me and slurped my dick up, going hard in the paint right a-fucking-way. There was no build up, no licking the shaft, and no massaging the balls. She went straight to it, letting my dick punch her tonsils. This wasn't going to take long at all. She pressed her fingers under my ball sack again, and just like I thought, I fired off without warning. This time, she let go, and that shit went all over her face. I watched her ass rub it in her skin like Mary Kay had come out with a skin probiotic that promised excellent results.

She licked her lips then rubbed them together like she had a lip balm on. I could feel more nut oozing out of my dick at the sight. That shit didn't get by her either. She went to it and sucked it right out of me. I almost screamed like a bitch. She had me squirming, trying to get away from her. When she released me, she said, "Now we can go take a shower."

---

WATCHING everybody devour the goulash Aunt Jen and Aunt Chrissy had made had my stomach fighting me. They made it just how I liked it too, without the elbow noodles. I didn't too much care for it with noodles. Felt like I was eating hamburger helper whenever I saw it that way. Although it nowhere near tasted the same, that was always the thought I got.

Goulash was nothing but a soupy dish with different types of meat and vegetables. It had beef meat, potatoes, carrots, and I wanted to believe they'd put deer meat and sausage in there too. I could only eat the damn juice, and that would be worse than me watching them enjoy it. That shit would tease me and make me wanna go home.

We were all at Jen and Chrissy's diner. Mr. Henderson said that would be better than gathering at his house. He had been staying with Aunt Chrissy and her husband because he said he could no longer sleep in that bed. I totally understood it. I had to get a new bed and rearrange my furniture after Tammy died, and she didn't die at my place. It had been three days since Grandma Henderson had died. Ty and Angel had gone home yesterday evening and promised to be back later today. I missed them something serious.

Aunt Jen and Aunt Chrissy had made enough goulash to feed all four hundred fifty people in Nome. Everyone was enjoying it while they talked and laughed like this was a family reunion. Before I got here, I'd gone by my property in Henderson Village to see how they were coming along. My guys had gotten all the cement poured, and we were just waiting for it to cure so a crew could come and frame the shit up.

They were insisting that they could start framing next week, but that would only be fourteen days. I told them they could either do what I said or kiss my ass. Twenty-eight days assured the concrete was cured enough. I didn't need any problems with my slab, especially since they poured it thick. My shit was seven inches instead of the minimum of four.

"So, since y'all are all here, there are some things we need to discuss about some things your mother put in place," Mr. Henderson said, gaining everyone's attention.

There were at least sixty to seventy people here. The kids and grandkids took up about forty-five of those people for sure. "When Joan was contemplating leaving me years ago, she bought all of you savings bonds. Those bonds have matured plus some. What I didn't know was that a couple of years later, she bought one for you too, Marcus."

Marcus's eyebrows lifted, and I could see that that bit of news affected him greatly. He closed his eyes and squeezed his baby girl that was seated on his lap as Syn rubbed his back. Grandpa nodded at Marcus and continued. "She also set up something for all the grandkids. W.J. and I will take care of that and make sure it's dispersed to all of you. She left plenty of other directives for when Nesha has the baby and when Jess gets married, but there was something else that I didn't know about."

Everyone looked on, waiting for him to reveal what Grandma had possibly hidden from him. "She had a stake in a business that has been extremely profitable. A few years back, she became the sole owner of a chain of furniture stores." He chuckled and shook his head slowly. "She wanted to make sure she was good after she left me. Although she never left, she still maintained her shares and went to meetings behind my back. There are twenty stores nationwide."

Storm stood from his seat. "She's the owner of Hilary's, isn't she?"

"Yeah. So, all of you that bought furniture from there were only investing into what is now yours. Your mother was a smart woman. I'm gonna miss her so much. The last few years have been our best years. I thought we would have more together, but God saw fit to take her now. I would have gladly gone first. I suppose since we've gotten right with Him, He decided it was time. I know this is hard for y'all, but it's extremely hard for me after over sixty years of marriage."

He fidgeted with his fingers for a minute then a slight smile made its way to his lips. "She also had some final things to say." He chuckled, and everyone's sad expressions turned into amused ones as they listened. "W.J., get ready to be a papa times two. She seems to think Tyeis is pregnant."

All eyes fell on me as I frowned. "She said that's why she's been giving you a hard time, Decaurey. Whether Tyeis knows it or not, she's pregnant."

"She's on birth control."

"Boy, don't argue with old folks' intuition. Have that woman take a test when she gets back," Grandpa said.

I was stunned. *Tyeis is pregnant?* As I pondered it over, Grandpa continued. "Jen, you get ready, because Jess is pregnant too."

I turned to her with my eyebrows lifted even higher as she leaned against Brix. She already knew, and so did Brix, obviously. "Jess! Did you tell Mama?" Aunt Jenahra asked.

Jess shook her head as tears spilled down her cheeks. "Brix and I found out the day before she passed away. When all this happened, I figured I would tell you guys later."

Aunt Jenahra ran over to her and hugged her tightly. When she did, Aunt Chrissy covered her ears, causing everyone to laugh. "Chrissy, you were her lap baby. No grandkids are on the way for you that she knows of, but she wants you to design furniture pieces for the store. She knows that you love that just as much as you love to cook, if not more."

Aunt Chrissy smiled and nodded. He was going down their list of kids from oldest to youngest, but I was still stuck on Tyeis being pregnant. "Your love is business. Start a consulting firm, helping other people get their businesses off the ground. Get Jasper to help you, because whether you realize it or not, Jasper looks up to you and tries to follow your path when it comes to business."

That was what Grandpa had said to Kenny. He had a couple of businesses, and so did Jasper. They were so smart when it came to running their shit. Chas barely had to get involved at all. "Jasper, yours was included with Kenny's, although you really need to consider opening a smoke and chill spot."

Jasper frowned and nodded. That shit would be right up his alley. Actually, I thought he was already considering it. "Tiff, you are fulfilling your destiny. You're teaching little girls to be proud of who they are and how to dominate in a male dominated sport. I'm proud of you, baby."

He'd read that one from a piece of paper. He was glancing at it the entire time, but I could tell he wasn't reading it word for word until he got to hers. He looked up at Storm and chuckled then went back to his paper. "Seven, calm your ass down, boy. Everybody is gonna vote for you. Let the last name speak for you."

Everybody laughed as Storm rolled his eyes. "I love that part of you though. Your straightforwardness can be a bit much at times, but don't change, baby. Before long, you may get hot wheels out of office."

I chuckled. She didn't need to pump Storm's head up any more than what it was. He didn't need to be thinking about the governor's seat, but here he was with his head tilted, staring up into the air. "Aww, hell no," Jasper said, causing everyone to crack up.

We thought he was finished, but he said, "Marcus, don't tell Storm, but you're my baby boy. CiCi was my best friend in grade school. We were so close. That's the version of her I chose to remember. You remind me so much of that version of her too. You are a hustler, and the way you fought for your daughter only caused me to admire you even more. Storm is gonna need a lot of help. You are just the man for the job. I love you."

Grandpa folded the piece of paper in his hand and took a deep breath. "The funeral is tomorrow and I'm not ready. I don't think I would have ever been ready. So tonight, I'm going to sleep in our bedroom to feel closer to her. I love y'all, and y'all continue to enjoy each other, but I'm going home."

KJ, Kenny's son, stood and helped him to his truck and let the family know that he would be staying there with him tonight. Everyone nodded in relief and went back to eating their food. I was still stuck. Jakari sat next to me. "What you think about what Grandma had to say?"

"Shit, nigga, I don't know. I'm still trying to process that shit. If she's pregnant, she can't know. She had to have gotten pregnant the first time we fucked. And she had to get pregnant from precum, because I fired off in the toilet."

"Damn. If she got pregnant back then, she has to be about four months along."

"She's gonna flip the fuck out, but I have to go get a pregnancy test before she gets here. Tyeis is almost forty, man. She said she was done having kids."

"What if she isn't pregnant?" he asked.

"Then we in the clear, but it's also something we need to talk about, because I wouldn't mind having one."

"Yeah, definitely something y'all need to talk about."

I nodded as Storm approached. "So you about to be a daddy. Make sure you get somebody to teach your baby how to fight."

"Maaaaan, shut up, fool!"

He cracked up laughing. "Well, if it's true, congratulations."

"Thanks, Storm."

I glanced over at Jess and told Jakari I would be right back. When I got to her, Shylou said, "Both of our premier full-figured models are pregnant. I guess we gotta work on a maternity line quick."

I chuckled and hugged Jess then shook Brixton's hand. "How far are you?"

"I don't know yet. I go to the doctor at the end of next week. I'll let you know."

I nodded. "Congratulations."

"Congratulations to you too. I'm here if you need me. I don't know how Tyeis is going to respond to that shit."

"I know. This could go either way, but I'll reach out if I need to, Jess. How crazy is it that we'll all be having kids at the same time? Jakari is the only one left out."

"Aye, I will gladly be left out this time," Jakari said from behind me.

We laughed about it, and as I was about to leave to head to the corner store, Uncle Kenny walked up on me and gave me two pregnancy tests. "I had them in the ambulance."

"Thanks, Unc. Pray my strength in the Lord."

He chuckled and shook his head then headed back over to talk to Jasper. They were already discussing how they could bring their mother's words to fruition. "Decaurey, bring yo' ass over here!" my mama yelled.

I knew her patience would start wearing thin. I purposely made her wait because of that. I chuckled as I made my way to her. "I'm gonna be a grandma times two? Two grandbabies at once?"

I chuckled. "I don't know if Grandma knew what she was talking about, but we gon' find out when Tyeis gets here. I'm glad she wasn't here to hear that. She would have had a whole meltdown."

"Well, thank God." She lifted her hand to my cheek. "I always knew you would be a good man for somebody's daughter. Although I wasn't feeling that shit with Tammy, I know you loved her. I was truly saddened when she died. Despite how I felt about the situation, it hurt when I found out about her diagnosis. I'm just happy that you have moved on in life and found someone else that you can love, and they can love you back. I see you have pregnancy tests."

"Yeah. Uncle Kenny gave them to me. Tyeis should be on her way now, so I'm going to text her and tell her to meet me at the house. We don't need to be around everybody when I ask her to take it."

My mama chuckled. "Right. I love you, baby. If it's positive, will you two come back out here?"

"It depends on how she responds. I love you, Ma."

"I love you more, baby. I can't wait until this mess is off your mouth."

"You? Me! *I* can't wait."

She laughed and hugged me then kissed my cheek. "Hopefully I'll see you when you get back."

I gave her a slight smile then said my goodbyes to everyone and headed out, trying to figure out how I would break this to Tyeis... nice and easy.

## CHAPTER TWENTY

### TYEIS

When Angel and I got to Decaurey's place in Beaumont, he was sitting there, looking to be in deep thought as we moved around, getting our things situated. We planned to stay a week, up until I had a shoot back in Houston for a local boutique. Once we were done getting things put away, I sat next to him on the couch.

"It's still early. You didn't want to go back to Nome and hang with everyone?"

"Well, I do, but I needed to speak to you privately first."

I immediately tensed up, and he noticed. "Umm... okay. Did I do something?"

"We both may have. Come to my bedroom, baby."

I supposed the term of endearment kind of calmed me down. He wouldn't have called me baby if he were upset with me about something. When he closed the door, he gestured for me to sit on the bed. I did so as he went to his dresser.

"I was in Nome earlier, and Grandpa addressed everyone with notes from Grandma... some of her last words to everyone. He went from person to person, but when he got to my dad, he told him he was about to have two grandchildren. My grandmother seems to think you're pregnant, baby."

I was staring at him in shock, and it seemed my breathing went on hiatus. He couldn't have said what I thought he said. I frowned slightly. "I'm on birth control. I didn't really care to have any more children. I mean..." I thought about what I was about to say. Decaurey was the man I loved. Things were different now. He sat next to me and grabbed my hand. I closed my eyes and said, "I would be willing to have your baby. I just don't think I'm ready right now."

"Have you missed a pill? She seemed to think your episodes were because you're pregnant. That would mean you're well into the pregnancy... if..."

His voice trailed off, and I knew what he was thinking. My breathing got heavier, and the tears started to fall. "You're the only one I've been having unprotected sex with. I know you may not believe that, but it's true. I can't even explain why I even allowed that to happen. You've never used a condom with me."

"Well, he said it in front of everyone, so Uncle Kenny gave me two pregnancy tests. You can take one now."

I nodded as I silently panicked. "Decaurey? What are we gonna do if I'm pregnant? How will we coparent, and what if—"

He literally clamped my lips shut with his thumb and pointer finger. I playfully slapped him on the arm as he chuckled. "Let's address all that after we find out the results of the test. Okay?"

"Okay."

I took a deep breath and grabbed the test from him. As I stood to go to his bathroom, he asked, "You want me to come in there with you?"

"No. I won't be able to pee with you watching me. I can't say I'm that comfortable yet."

He slowly shook his head. When I got inside the bathroom and had closed the door, I set the test on the countertop and silently prayed that this shit came up negative. What the hell did she know anyway? How in the fuck was I gonna have a fupa tuck and titty lift if I was pregnant? This couldn't be happening to me. I felt like I was having a meltdown.

The door opened, and Decaurey walked in. He stood behind me and slid his arms around my waist. "If you're pregnant, I'm going to be here for you. You know that. I'm going to be here if you aren't. You won't have to do this alone. If I have to move you here, I will. They will be framing my house up in two weeks. It won't be long before it's done. Ty, you and Angel are my family, baby. I'm pretty sure it will be a challenge with your illness and medication, but we'll figure it out together. Yo' sandman ain't gon' let you down."

I smiled at him through the mirror then huffed and opened the box. He knew I was in here panicking. It was crazy just how well he knew me. "How did you know I was in here panicking?"

"I didn't. But I knew you weren't in here pissing."

I frowned. "How?"

"Girl, I can hear when you pissing. That big, juicy ass clit you got pack some pressure."

Now I was embarrassed. I turned away from him. "If you don't stop tripping and take this test. Either way, we gon' still be together… just one person heavier."

He kissed my head and left the bathroom. I was doing my best to stay calm, but it wasn't happening. Despite my panicked state, I sat on the toilet and pissed on the stick. I covered it with the cap and finished my business, then washed my hands. By the time I was done, Decaurey was knocking on the door. "Come in," I said quietly.

I couldn't even look at the test. My stomach felt like it was in knots. "Baby?"

"Huh?"

"You're pregnant. Those lines are both bright pink."

My body betrayed my thoughts, and I broke down crying. Decaurey scooped me up like a baby and carried me to his bed. He gently wiped my tears away and kissed me repeatedly. "Look at me, baby."

I lifted my eyes to his. "You have nothing to worry about. You and your best friend will be in this together."

I frowned. "Jess is pregnant?"

"Yep. Grandma revealed that too. The only difference was that Jess and Brix already knew. They just hadn't announced it yet. So you won't be alone. We have a huge family, and everyone is willing to help out and support us, especially my mama. Nesha has her mother, so she rarely calls my mama for anything. She's too excited, so I'm sure she will be there for you if I can't be for whatever reason."

I closed my eyes and took deep breaths. When I opened them, he was staring at me with a slight smile on his face. "Let's go to Nome," I said.

He smiled bigger. "I'm gonna be a daddy, Ty."

He was so happy. I still wasn't feeling it, but whether I was or not, I'd better get ready for this restroom-stall baby. "Your shit must be potent. I had to have gotten pregnant from your prenut."

"Hell yeah. Like Day 26 said, I must got that babymaker."

I chuckled. "So, should I get a doctor in Beaumont or Houston?"

"Honestly, although Beaumont would be convenient, I would much rather you get one in Houston."

"Good. We're on the same page with that then," I said as he put his shoes on.

He walked over to me and asked, "You wanna tell Angel?"

"Of course."

He led me to the front room where Angel was seated watching an old episode of *Demon Slayer*. "Angel, I have... I mean, we have something to tell you."

She turned off the TV and turned to look at us. Her eyebrows lifted and she asked, "Are y'all getting married? Is Decaurey gonna be my dad?"

Decaurey chuckled and answered for me. "One day, I will marry your mother, and I can be your dad whenever you want me to be. You don't have to wait until we're married. That's not what we have to tell you though."

I stared at him, wondering how he could be so confident in us. I wished I could just go with the flow like he did. I was trying my hardest though. He wrapped his arms around me and kissed my cheek. "I'm pregnant, Angel. You're going to have a sister or brother."

I sounded like a whole ass fool. How did I not know I was pregnant? Four fucking months at that! There was no way Decaurey's grandmother would be able to sense I was pregnant after a week or two. Angel's eyes widened, then a big smile broke out on her face. "I'm going to be a big sister and a babysitter!"

I closed my eyes, and the biggest smile broke out on my face too. Angel could make anyone smile. She giggled and caused me to giggle as well. I turned to Decaurey and kissed his lips. We were going to be a family, and I was now looking forward to it.

---

"DON'T WORRY. We can go to the same doctor and do this together. I think you might be further along than me, but I will be there with you every step of the way."

I smiled at Jess as she rubbed my stomach. No one could tell that I was pregnant. That shit was strange to me. Maybe this hanging pouch hid it. My body was a lot tighter when I got pregnant with Angel. I rubbed her belly, too, and apparently, Nesha got jealous, so she came over for us to rub her belly. We all laughed. I felt a lot better, so I was happy that we came to Nome. Although tomorrow would be a sad occasion, I was happy to be here with my girls.

Decaurey appeared behind me, wrapping his arms around my waist. He was being so affectionate with me. He was always affectionate, but he was even more so now. "Baby, my mama wanted to talk to you."

I smiled at him. "Okay."

He led me to his mother, and the minute her eyes met mine, she smiled so big, putting my soul at ease. When I got close, she pulled me into her arms and hugged me tight. "Tyeis, I'm so happy I don't know what to do with myself. I just want you to know that I'm here for whatever you need, even if it's just for you to vent. I literally follow W.J. around all day. I'm sure he will be glad that I found someone else to occupy my time. Just let me know whatever you need. I want to make this transition as easy as possible for you."

I smiled at her and hugged her again. She felt like a mother should. My mother had been gone for a long time due to a car accident, and I missed the way it felt to have someone in your corner, showing genuine love and support. "Thank you. I'm going to need all the help I can get," I said as she giggled.

She grabbed my hand and took me toward the kitchen to get something to eat. I glanced back at Decaurey to see the biggest smile on his face. As she fixed me a bowl of what looked to be some kind of soup or stew, I decided to be open with her. Being with Decaurey had taught me to be more transparent about my condition. Whoever didn't want to be around me because of it, wasn't supposed to be around me in the first place.

"Mrs. Olivia, you should know that I have bipolar disorder. So if sometimes I seem off, I probably am."

She smiled at me then lifted her eyebrows as if what I said was no big deal. "Okay. And? We're family, and we're here to help each other through challenges... whatever that may look like from person to person. Decaurey loves you and so does Jess, Jenahra, Shylou, and Carter. That's good enough for me, baby."

I released the breath I seemed to be holding. This was definitely meant to be. However, when I saw Storm approaching, I wanted to roll my eyes. Just from the smirk on his lips, I knew he was coming with the foolishness. "It still ain't too late to change your mind and run."

"Run from who? You?" I asked, and he laughed.

"Shiiiid, you shol right! Make sure you know what the fuck you getting into associating yourself with the Storm, baby girl. These winds don't ever take a break!"

I laughed so loud I damn near scared myself. "I think I'm in good company. We can be on bullshit together, Uncle Mayor."

"Hell yeah. Decaurey picked the right one. He better be careful though. You seem like a shit starter like me. Hopefully he learn to just surrender before it even start."

I laughed again as Mrs. Olivia said, "You gon' get off my baby, Storm. Go find you something else to do."

Storm gave her a one-cheeked smile, then looked at me, gesturing with his two fingers, saying 'we here' or that we're on the same page.

I slowly shook my head as he walked away. "I can see it now. Things are going to get extremely interesting and fun with you around."

I smiled big. She had no fucking idea.

## CHAPTER TWENTY-ONE

### DECAUREY

"He's out of jail and back in Houston, laying low. Bitch ass nigga need to stay that way if he knows what's good for him."

Jakari was giving all of us an update on Tyrese. We'd decided to meet at the barbershop again. It had been a few days since the funeral, and unfortunately, we were all having to figure out how to go through our day to day without Grandma. It wasn't as difficult for me since I didn't see her every day, but for her kids, it was a lot harder.

Her homegoing celebration was beautiful. Kenny and Storm had both talked. Kenny talked about her caring and sensitive side, while Storm talked about her being a firecracker. Both of their talks were great. Kenny could barely keep it together when he spoke about her love for Kendrick. It was like he was reliving the death of his son because of Grandma's final words to him. I knew he would get through it with the help of his wife and the entire family.

Grandpa had been cooped up in the house since the funeral, not wanting to leave their bedroom, so everyone vowed to check on him every day, making sure he ate and was tended to. KJ and Jakari's brother, Christian, had been staying there. Hell, the house was big enough for a damn army to stay there. It had about ten bedrooms. That was the only time the Hendersons really flaunted their money when it wasn't business related: their houses. Everyone's houses were amazing.

Pop had said that he had the smallest house of everyone, but he changed that a couple of years ago. He said he had to make room for whenever he started having grandchildren. Now he had two on the way. It was still hard for me to believe that Ty was pregnant. I was even more grateful she didn't panic nearly as much as I thought she would. Seeing all the support she had was what kept her calm. I knew she still had worries, but I planned to soothe them all as best I could.

"Well, the first time he feel froggy and decide to leap, I'm gon' be right there with my net to cut his fucking legs off to deep fry them shits," Philly said, causing everybody to chuckle.

"I'm just glad that we may not have to worry about him. Ty and Angel will be moving out here soon, so I can keep a better eye on them. They leave to go home tomorrow, and that shit got me on edge," I added.

"You ain't got shit to worry about," Jakari said. "I got protection for them. You ever heard of Watchful Eyes out of Beaumont? They gon' take care of them. They'll take care of him, too, if we wanna keep our hands clean. I think it will be a great partnership to establish. They do security for large events as well."

"Hmm. That sounds like a good partnership to form, Jakari," Pop said. "That's boss moves."

"Thanks, J. I appreciate that. That gives me some relief. What's the name of the ones that will specifically be looking out for them?"

"So far, I believe it's a nigga named Seneca and another that goes by Jungle."

"With names like that, I have to assume they're the real deal," I said with a slight chuckle.

We continued to talk more, but my mind was long gone from here. It was on Tyeis and how I planned to cater to her every need tonight. She'd gotten an appointment with the same doctor Jess was using in Houston. They considered her pregnancy high risk, so they wanted to get her in as soon as possible, especially because we thought she was so far along.

She didn't even realize that she hadn't had a cycle in three months. She said that she used to be irregular, and certain medications had made it worse, but for the last year, she had been having one monthly. So, I supposed when she didn't have one, she didn't think it was anything crucial enough to look into.

Angel had been doing great out here. She had really bonded with Maui, Milana, Malia, Ashanni, and Karima. They were all close in age, except for Malia. She was a few years under them. Karima was a few years older, and she looked at all of them as her little sisters, since they were the rodeo crew.

Angel was already expressing an interest in going to one to see them compete. Karima did it full time, along with her brother KJ. Milana was working on it. Once she graduated high school, it would really be her time. I told her I would be glad to take her to one, especially since they had one coming up soon in Fort Worth. Malachi would be there putting on a fucking show.

Tonight would be time for Tyeis and I to bond even more. I was finally ready to show her romance. I'd made reservations at J. Wilson's and had planned to take her to a wine tasting afterward. She wasn't a big alcohol drinker, but I knew she sipped wine every now and then. However, I had to change those plans because I'd forgotten that fast she was pregnant. I didn't know how I could forget about my seed though. *Pure craziness.*

Storm was on the floor, talking about the damn election coming up in a couple of weeks. Marcus was standing beside him, and surprisingly, no one was laughing or ignoring him. Everyone was tuned in and listening to what he needed from us. He was pretty serious about everything he was saying until Jasper said, "Storm, Abney still ain't running. You are by yourself. If he hasn't thrown his hat in by now, he's not going to. Matter of fact, I think it's too late for him to do so anyway. You a shoe in, nigga. I told you this shit before."

Storm stared at him for a minute, then a slight smile graced his lips. "You know what? I think the deadline did pass for him to announce he's running, but you know these white people out here think they running shit and are above the fucking law. Let me look up the rules right quick."

Jasper rolled his eyes as Storm did some shit on his phone. Marcus was right beside him, doing shit on his phone too. *Hmm.* Maybe they would be good for Nome. The elementary school in Henderson Village would get finished and so would the new post office. Marcus gave Storm his phone, and a frown graced his face. "It's one fucking week. So he still has a week to decide. That's some country shit right there. In other cities, that shit has to be done like forty-five days in advance... so a month and a half."

"Storm, out of nearly five hundred people eligible to vote, you don't need that much time to campaign. Everybody already knows everybody," Uncle Kenny said.

"That's where you're wrong. Those muthafuckas don't know me like they think they do. They about to find out though when I win this election."

"A'ight, y'all. It's good catching up, but I gotta go take care of my baby. Uncle Mayor, I got'chu for whatever you need."

Jakari smirked at me. Calling him that shit buttered him up, and he lost all train of thought. I witnessed it when Jess and Tyeis called him that. He smiled slightly. "A'ight, nephew. Take care of my crazy ass niece and tell her to call me."

I frowned. Before I could ask why, he said, "See, you already worried about the wrong shit. I'm doing this for Aspen, so mind your business."

I shook my head and told everyone I would see them later and headed out to make my baby's day.

---

"DECAUREY, this is nice, baby. Thank you."

I nodded as I smiled at her. She'd gotten some dish called Man Candy and that shit looked good as hell. Here I was sitting here with some mashed potatoes, mad as hell. Her dish was some kind of pork with what she called a spicy jelly. That shit had my mouth watering. I looked at the menu to see it was a slow smoked pork belly tossed in habanero jelly. I'd get some wire cutters and cut all this shit loose for a taste of that.

"I know this is torture for you, but we will definitely have to come back when you're done with that wire."

"Yeah. You enjoy yourself though. I can't wait for your appointment. They will probably be able to tell us the sex too if you're as far along as we think you are."

"Right. I'm starting to get excited. Your mom probably has me that way. She's beyond excited too. I know how to handle girls, but if our baby is a boy, he will be all yours when he becomes a toddler."

I chuckled. "I don't mind that shit at all. I'm excited too. It's still somewhat surreal. I wasn't expecting us to be here already. This moved a lot faster than I expected, but I'm not upset about that shit either. I'm a fast mover when I know something is right. Although you were just wanting what was swinging between my legs, you intrigued me. Because of how we met and what went down, I thought we would move slower, especially when I didn't see yo' ass for three months."

She laughed. "How did you think we would move slower after you fucked me in a bathroom stall, Decaurey? That was wishful thinking. After experiencing all this, there was no way you would be able to slow down. That was why I stayed away to make sure I knew what I was doing."

"Cocky ass," I mumbled. "You right though. That pussy swallowed my hopes and dreams then spit that shit back at me. After the second time, I wanted to slide a ring on your finger until you had a meltdown on me because of the insomnia. I'm so glad you came back though. We probably wouldn't be here if you hadn't."

"Stubborn, spoiled ass," she said as she cut her eyes playfully. "I'm glad too, baby. I suppose I would have had to come back at some point when I would have realized I was pregnant. I still can't believe that I didn't know I was pregnant. This shit is baffling to me."

"Well, it doesn't matter now. We will be excellent parents. I meant what I said to Angel the other day. I plan to make you my wife."

"I know, and I'm still overwhelmed by it. Someone wants to marry Tyeis Warner. What the fuck?"

She giggled as I stared at her seriously. I gently slid my fingers down her exposed shoulder and arm. "First of all, you fine as fuck. That feisty ass attitude is a turn on like no other. You're smart, independent, and you're an amazing mother. I want you to know that your challenges and issues are no longer your own. Whatever you're facing is now *our* problems... *our* challenges... *our* issues. I love you, and I got you and our kids for life."

I watched her facial expression soften and her eyes water. She grabbed my hand and kissed it, then held it to her face. "Stop talking to me like that before you end up taking me in the restroom here. I'm not wearing panties. This dress gon' be wet as fuck in a minute. Chill out, sandman."

I gave her a slow smile and nodded. She had me wanting to do just what she said. She didn't know it yet, but she was gon' be riding this dick before we left. I had no plans after this, because the painting with a twist would be closed by the time we left. I was more than sure she wouldn't be disappointed when this hammer started knocking holes in her walls.

I sipped some water to wet my lips then put more ChapStick on them. "See, you using that cheap shit. Remind me to give you some of what one of the models made for us. That shit will be good on your lips all day, no matter what."

She was trying to change the subject to calm her pussy down. I was cool with it for now. We continued eating... her pork belly and my mashed potatoes, then I took care of the bill, and we headed to the Tahoe. When I opened the back door, she frowned. After looking around, she got in without taking a second look. I got in behind her and immediately unfastened and unzipped my pants, pulling my dick from my drawers. She was about to put her mouth on him, but I stopped her. "Naw. I need to feel that slick pussy. We can do all that other shit when we get home. Come fuck yo' nigga, Tyeis."

A soft moan left her lips, and she lifted her dress then straddled me, dropping that sweet, pregnant pussy right where it was needed. "Ooooh fuuuuck," I groaned.

I slumped a little in the seat as she rolled her hips while staring into my eyes. "I love you, Decaurey."

"Mm hmm. Now show me," I said, then smacked her ass.

She started bouncing her ass on me, pulling my dick with every stroke. My head dropped back to the seat as I rested my hands at her hips. When my eyes closed, I could feel her lean over closer to me and kiss my lips. "Look at me. Watch me fuck you, Decaurey."

I opened my eyes to stare at her. Her lips parted and a sweet moan left her thick lips. She pulled her dress over her head, and my gaze went right to the action, watching her pussy slide up and down my dick, leaving its essence all over it. I could feel it on my balls. She knew what her loving did to me. She could leave me speechless, just like I could leave her. We were a perfect match.

I sat up and sucked her nipples, and her hands went to the back of my head as she continued bouncing her hips on me. "Decaurey! I'm about to cum! Shiiiit!"

I glanced around the vehicle to make sure no one was near, because I would never live this shit down if any of those Hendersons had to come get us out of jail. I began lifting my hips to fuck her back and hurry my nut along so we could get home. I needed to kiss her pussy and take my time with it.

Her pussy unleashed its love for me everywhere while she leaned over and bit my fucking shoulder. Wrapping my arms around her waist, I went to work in that pussy. If she wasn't already pregnant, she would have been sure to get pregnant with this one right here in my Tahoe. "I love you, Ty. Fuck!"

I blasted off in her depths, trembling like a crack fiend that finally got his fix. "Got damn, baby."

Neither of us made a move to get home. I was stuck for the moment, and it appeared she was too as she laid her head on my shoulder, not saying a word. I turned to her and kissed her head. "Come on, baby. If you wanna stay naked, just stay back here and lay across the seat. I gotta get us home."

She lifted her head and licked her lips, then fell to the seat. I smirked at her and pulled my pants up. When I got out, I saw her stretching out across the seat. I didn't know how I was gonna fucking concentrate while she was sprawled across the back seat buckid nekkid. When I got in the driver's seat, I didn't waste any time taking off for my place. We were about ten minutes away.

When I got to the red light on Gladys and Dowlen, I heard her moan. I turned to look at her, and she was laid across the seat, legs spread, and finger fucking herself. "Ty, what the fuck you doing?"

She glanced at me then sat up, turning her body to face me, and spread her legs where I could really see her fucking herself. Her juices mixed with my nut were dripping from her fingers to the seat. She took the cake when she withdrew them and brought them to her mouth. I damn near blasted off in my pants. "Any more questions, sandman?"

I was mesmerized as she slowly pushed them back inside of her while pinching her nipple with her other hand. The blaring horns behind me got my attention, and I got to my place in record time. When I parked, I turned to her. "I'm gon' fuck the shit out of you for that."

"You promise?"

"Take that shit to the fucking bank."

## CHAPTER TWENTY-TWO

### TYEIS

"What did they say? How far along are you?" I asked Jess as she made her way back up front.

"I'm ten weeks. Seeing the baby on the ultrasound screen pulled the tears out of me, but hearing the baby's heartbeat had me damn near bawling. I've always wanted to have a family, but having one with Brix is fairytalish. Wow," she said as a tear fell down her cheek.

Brix kissed her tenderly as they went to the waiting area. After our appointments, we were going to this restaurant for lunch. I wanted some oxtails so bad. Decaurey was still a little salty because his mouth was wired shut, but he promised me that no matter what, I could have whatever I wanted.

The nurse had already taken my vitals, and I'd offered a urine sample. We were just waiting for them to prepare the room for me. Decaurey brought his hand to my stomach and rubbed it. He'd been somewhat quiet. I knew he was nervous, because I was too. I supposed we expressed our nerves in different ways. I talked *too* much and couldn't be still when I was nervous. He was the opposite, quiet and motionless.

"Ms. Warner, you can come in the room now."

I looked up to see the nurse smiling at me. Decaurey quickly stood and helped me from my seat. When I stood, I felt a fucking kick. My eyes widened as I stared at him. "The baby kicked."

He smiled big. That alone let me know I was just as far along as his grandmother thought. I walked inside the room, and the nurse closed the door after telling me to disrobe and put a gown on. Decaurey was still smiling, and that made my spirit light. "What are you thinking?" he asked.

"That I'm ready to see our baby... the baby we made in lust in the hip hop club's restroom."

He laughed. "It don't even matter where he or she was conceived. Our baby will be raised in love."

He stood from his seat and helped me get my gown on. "You know I can tell that you're pregnant now. From the moment we confirmed it, I started paying even closer attention to your body. You're carrying the weight in your breasts and ass. That's why we never noticed. I can see it in your belly now though. Plus, I've gained ten pounds. How the fuck when I've been eating mashed potatoes, soup, and drinking liquids?"

"Well, you probably gained more than that and started losing some after the fight. Weigh yourself again next week, and I bet you will be down more weight."

"If you say so," he said as he helped me back on the table. "How are you feeling?"

"I feel fine. When I was pregnant with Angel, I stayed sick as a dog."

"Probably because you were stressed. Weren't you in school?"

"Yeah, and it didn't help that her father was on my last fucking nerve. He better be glad he's not answering my calls. I was gonna cuss his ass smooth the fuck out for the way he talked to my baby and hurt her feelings. That's why he's avoiding me. He's probably blocked me. Jackass."

Decaurey only chuckled and rubbed my belly more, making sure I remained calm. When the doctor came in, he took a seat. "Hello, Ms. Warner! I'm Doctor Rusk. I'm so glad to have you on as a patient. So, you are indeed pregnant. We are going to do an ultrasound to see if we can tell how far along you are. You look to be in the early stages, but I noticed on your paperwork that it's been four months since your last menstrual. So we definitely need to get on the ball to see what we're looking at. The ultrasound tech will take care of you."

The minute she said that, the tech walked in and had me lay flat. Decaurey came on the other side of me, prepared to see our bundle of joy. My hands were trembling, because suddenly, I'd gotten nervous. It seemed my man could sense it. He grabbed my hand and gently caressed it. "It's okay, baby."

He leaned over and kissed my lips as the tech smiled and proceeded to put gel on my belly. I anxiously stared at the screen, waiting for what I would see. When she put the wand to my stomach, I immediately heard a lot of noise, but as my eyes focused on what I was seeing, I nearly lost my mind… the little bit I had left after finding out I was having a baby at damn near forty years old.

"There they are! Do you want to know the sex of the babies?"

Decaurey's smile was the biggest I'd ever seen it as the tears sprang from my eyes. I said through my tears, "Yes."

"Okay. Baby A, right here," she said, using the pointer to indicate which one she was referring to, "is a boy! Baby B is a sweet little princess. You are about eighteen weeks along."

"Wait 'til I tell my mama. She gon' be as happy as I am. How are you feeling, baby?"

"A little overwhelmed."

"Look at me." I lifted my eyes to his brown ones. "You ain't got shit to worry about. I'm gonna make shit as easy as I can for you. If I have to hire a maid and a cook, you got that. Whatever you need."

I smiled at him and brought my hand to his cheek as the tech walked out. He grabbed my hand and kissed it, then smiled again.

"Wait 'til I tell Storm. He ain't the only one with bionic sperm that can produce twins."

I chuckled because I could hear Storm saying some shit like that. *Twins*. What was I gonna do with twins? Decaurey did his best to calm my nerves, but I couldn't seem to chill out. When the doctor came in, she said, "Wow! Congratulations, you two!"

I smiled slightly as Decaurey held my hand between his, still caressing it. "You gon' be fine, baby, I promise."

---

AFTER MY APPOINTMENT, we joined Jess and Brix for lunch. My visit took forever, because all sorts of tests had to be run to check for birth defects or anything else abnormal. Jess and Brix were the first ones to know we were expecting twins. Jess nearly blew my eardrum out with how excited she was. Once we got back from Houston, I told Angel, and she was beyond excited. She'd stayed here in Nome with Tiffany and Ryder to spend time with Milana.

My nerves had calmed once we left the doctor's office, so I was just as excited. I was about to be the mother of three. Mrs. Olivia and Mr. W.J. were so excited and couldn't wait to start planning for the babies. Nesha had found out she was having a boy, so knowing he would have two grandsons was the icing on the cake, especially since he had all girls. Mrs. Olivia had promised that she would be there for me every step of the way.

Knowing that I had such a strong support system made me feel complete and the happiest I'd been. I knew there would be challenges to overcome and issues to resolve, but I was ready to face all of it head on. I just wished Decaurey's grandmother was here so we could tell her just how right she was.

Decaurey had told me that Storm wanted me to call him. When I did, he asked for us to come over to his home. He said Aspen wanted to talk to me about some things. I wasn't sure what she wanted to talk about, but I was ready to lend my ear. When we drove in the driveway, his youngest son appeared on the screen. Decaurey said, "What's up, Remy? Tell your dad to open the gate."

Remy frowned and asked, "Why? He didn't say we were having company! That mean you didn't ask to come over here!"

The screen went dark, and I chuckled. "I can't stand his bad ass kids, I swear!" Decaurey said, then laughed.

He loved those bad ass kids, and that was why he was laughing about it. He called Storm to tell him to open the gate, and within a few seconds, we were granted access. Decaurey parked then walked around to help me out. Before we could get to the door, Storm had opened it. "Remy is mayor secret service. I forgot to tell him to expect y'all."

When Storm laughed, I laughed too. "Y'all come in. How was the doctor's appointment?"

Decaurey frowned at him. "How you know she had a doctor's appointment?"

"First of all, nigga, it's my job to know the comings and goings of people in my family. Secondly, you about to be a citizen in my town. If I don't know, you must be extremely secretive, and that would be a problem if you wanna live in Big City Nome. Plus, your loud-mouth father is way too proud to keep shit to himself."

Decaurey rolled his eyes then smiled immediately. "Well, she's eighteen weeks. Grandma was right on the money, but there was something Grandma failed to mention." He pulled me in his arms as Aspen joined us. "We're having twins. You ain't the only one that can produce multiples. I almost wish she was having triplets so I could throw that in your face."

Storm frowned then hesitantly extended his hand to congratulate me but never took his eyes off Decaurey. "Congrats, Ty. I'm gon' let you go on with Aspen so you can be out of dodge before I hem yo' nigga up."

Aspen giggled and grabbed my hand, pulling me to what I

learned was her office upon entry. She sat on the couch and offered for me to sit as well. "Congratulations on your babies!"

"Thank you."

I wasn't real familiar with her, so I was a little on edge about what she had to say. It didn't help when she said, "I hope what I want to ask you to do doesn't offend you. I probably shouldn't even know this information. Storm told me you were bipolar. I recently started a segment for an online magazine about mental illness and health. I would love for you to be a part."

I was just staring at her. "How does Storm know?"

"Did you hear his explanation a little while ago? I have no idea, but apparently, he was right."

"Yeah. I umm... I haven't been fully transparent about it."

"Oh. I'm sorry. I just thought that people hearing it from someone in their position could be beneficial. You telling them treatments that have worked for you or certain activities you engage in that help would be received way better coming from a credible source. I can only make recommendations based on research. They say experience is the best teacher. You're experienced on the subject. Please say you'll think about it?"

I fidgeted with my fingers for a moment and remembered how free I felt when Decaurey knew. Maybe I would feel the same way if I stopped hiding from the world and embraced who I was as an individual. I lifted my head and stared into her eyes. "I'll do it. Just tell me what you need."

She smiled big as she pushed her green-rimmed glasses up on the bridge of her nose, causing me to do the same to my glasses. "Thank you so much! Yes! You are about to make a difference in so many lives. I can feel it."

"I'm glad you're confident about that, because I'm not."

She pulled me from my seat and hugged me. "I am confident, and eventually, you will be too."

She led me back to the front area where Decaurey was arm wrestling with their older son, pretending it was a struggle. When Storm noticed us, he stood. "Are y'all staying for dinner?"

"No. Decaurey still can't eat. Plus, we need to pick up Angel from Tiffany's. Thank you, Uncle Mayor, for offering."

He chuckled. "Just make sure y'all watching the election so y'all can be at headquarters, ready to turn up."

"Lawd have mercy. I'll be glad when this election is over," Decaurey said after huffing.

Storm pushed his head. "It's only gonna get worse when I get elected. You think I'm in your shit now? You have no fucking idea."

Decaurey pulled me out of the house as Storm laughed. "Bye, y'all!" Aspen yelled.

We gave her a wave. Once we were inside the SUV, I told Decaurey what Aspen wanted. He was surprised, but I could see the pride fill his chest when I said I agreed to do it. He grabbed my hand. "I'm so proud of you, baby. In the past couple of months, I've seen so much positive change in you. I love it, and I'm glad you're my woman."

I could feel my face heat up. "No one has expressed being proud of me since my dad was alive. Decaurey, you are everything God meant for me to have. I'm so glad we found one another. I never thought having a man like you was possible."

He smiled as his face reddened a bit. I grabbed his hand as he pulled out of the driveway to the street. This couldn't be reality. God had blessed my daughter and me immensely. It had to be a dream, and I never wanted to wake up from it.

"I'm glad you didn't walk away for good. Love is always possible when two people are willing to put in the work to make it worth it."

*Yep. This has to be a dream... a damn good one.*

## The End

If you did not read the author's note at the beginning, please go back and do so before leaving a review. 😊

## FROM THE AUTHOR...

Whew! It's done for now. This story will pick up almost where it left off in Jakari's book. You will get to learn more about the relationships and pending babies on the horizon.

Tyeis almost messed around and lost something special. However, mental illness is a real thing, and it's sad we're still having to say this in 2023, especially with all the resources available. I loved her relationship with her daughter, Angel. She kept her in pocket for the most part. Angel didn't know anything was supposed to be a secret, and I was grateful that Tyeis understood that about her daughter and how down syndrome affected her.

Decaurey was everything I expected him to be and more. At the beginning, I thought he was going to prove me wrong and be an ass, but he rectified that quickly. He was everything Tyeis needed, and I was happy about that, because I was thinking the worst for a minute.

Of course, Storm was Storm. The family never disappointed. However, when Grandma Henderson died, the hardest part for me to write was her words to Kenny. The minute he revealed what she said and did, the tears fell from my eyes without warning. That baby's death still bothers me.

## FROM THE AUTHOR...

In the next book, you will find out whether Storm has opposition or not. If Abney tries to run, Storm is gonna have a whole fit and could probably blow all of Nome off the damn map. LOL! Of all my characters, he's one that constantly speaks to me, no matter whose story I'm writing. So I know he's not going to let me rest too long before starting Jakari's story to update you on the family and what everyone is doing. I'm already hearing his disdain with me pulling the "Bee-Nots" into the Henderson Family Saga (Inside joke with Monica's Romantic Sweet Spot). SMH!

I truly hope that you enjoyed this drama-filled ride that probably had your feelings all over the place. As always, I gave it my all. Whether you liked it or not, please take the time to leave a review on Amazon and/or Goodreads and wherever else this book is sold.

There's also an amazing playlist on Apple Music and Spotify for this book, under the same title that includes some great R&B tracks to tickle your fancy.

Please keep up with me on Facebook, Instagram, and TikTok (@authormonicawalters), Twitter (@monlwalters), and Clubhouse (@monicawalters). You can also visit my Amazon author page at www.amazon.com/author/monica.walters to view my releases.

Please subscribe to my webpage for updates and sneak peeks of upcoming releases! https://authormonicawalters.com.

For live discussions, giveaways, and inside information on upcoming releases, join my Facebook group, Monica's Romantic Sweet Spot at https://bit.ly/2P2lo6X.

# OTHER TITLES BY MONICA WALTERS

### **Standalones**

Love Like a Nightmare

Forbidden Fruit (An Erotic Novella)

Say He's the One

Only If You Let Me (a spin-off of Say He's the One)

On My Way to You (An Urban Romance)

Any and Everything for Love

Savage Heart (A KeyWalt Crossover Novel with Shawty You for Me by T. Key)

I'm In Love with a Savage (A KeyWalt Crossover Novel with Trade It All by T. Key)

Don't Tell Me No (An Erotic Novella)

To Say, I Love You: A Short Story Anthology with the Authors of BLP

Drive Me to Ecstasy

Whatever It Takes: An Erotic Novella

When You Touch Me

When's the Last Time?

Best You Ever Had

Deep As It Goes (A KeyWalt Crossover Novel with Perfect Timing by T. Key)

The Shorts: A BLP Anthology with the Authors of BLP (Made to Love You- Collab with Kay Shanee)

All I Need is You (A KeyWalt Crossover Novel with Divine Love by T. Key)

This Love Hit Different (A KeyWalt Crossover Novel with Something New by T. Key)

Until I Met You

Marry Me Twice

Last First Kiss (a spin-off of Marry Me Twice)

Nobody Else Gon' Get My Love (A KeyWalt Crossover Novel with Better Than Before by T. Key)

Love Long Overdue (A KeyWalt Crossover Novel with Distant Lover by T. Key)

Next Lifetime

Fall Knee-Deep In It

Unwrapping Your Love: The Gift

Who Can I Run To

You're Always on My Mind (a spin-off of Who Can I Run To)

Stuck On You

Full Figured 18 with Treasure Hernandez (Love Won't Let Me Wait)

It's Just a Date: A Billionaire Baby Romance

You Make Me Feel (a spin-off of Stuck On You) (coming soon!)

## **The Sweet Series**

Bitter Sweet

Sweet and Sour

Sweeter Than Before

Sweet Revenge

Sweet Surrender

Sweet Temptation

Sweet Misery

Sweet Exhale

Never Enough (A Sweet Series Update)

### **Sweet Series: Next Generation**

Can't Run From Love

Access Denied: Luxury Love

Still: Your Best

### **Sweet Series: Kai's Reemergence**

Beautiful Mistake

Favorite Mistake

### **Motives and Betrayal Series**

Ulterior Motives

Ultimate Betrayal

Ultimatum: #lovemeorleaveme, Part 1

Ultimatum: #lovemeorleaveme, Part 2

### **Written Between the Pages Series**

The Devil Goes to Church Too

The Book of Noah (A KeyWalt Crossover Novel with The Flow of Jah's Heart by T. Key)

The Revelations of Ryan, Jr. (A KeyWalt Crossover Novel with All That Jazz by T. Key)

The Rebirth of Noah

### **Behind Closed Doors Series**

Be Careful What You Wish For

You Just Might Get It

Show Me You Still Want It

## The Country Hood Love Stories

8 Seconds to Love

Breaking Barriers to Your Heart

Training My Heart to Love You

## The Country Hood Love Stories: The Hendersons

Blindsided by Love

Ignite My Soul

Come and Get Me

In Way Too Deep

You Belong to Me

Found Love in a Rider

Damaged Intentions: The Soul of a Thug

Let Me Ride

Better the Second Time Around

I Wish I Could Be The One

I Wish I Could Be The One 2

Put That on Everything: A Henderson Family Novella

What's It Gonna Be?

Someone Like You (2nd Generation story)

A Country Hood Christmas with the Hendersons

Where Is the Love (2nd Generation story)

## The Berotte Family Series

Love On Replay

Deeper Than Love

Something You Won't Forget

I'm The Remedy

Love Me Senseless

I Want You Here

Don't Fight The Feeling

When You Dance

I'm All In

Give Me Permission

Force of Nature

Say You Love Me

Where You Should Be

Hard To Love

Made in the USA
Coppell, TX
20 February 2025